P9-CBG-546

*Somewhere Near Paradise*

**Other Avalon Books by Marjorie Everitt**

*COUNTRY BLUES*
*SWEET DREAMS, SERENA*
*RIVER OF STARS*
*A TOUCH OF HONEY*
*DANGER AT DEMON'S COVE*
*SECRETS OF ROSEMANOR*

WATERLOO HIGH SCHOOL LIBRARY
1464 INDUSTRY RD.
ATWATER, OHIO 44201

# Somewhere Near Paradise

✳

## Marjorie Everitt

Fic
EVE

# AVALON BOOKS

THOMAS BOUREGY AND COMPANY, INC.
401 LAFAYETTE STREET
NEW YORK, NEW YORK 10003

© Copyright 1992 by Marjorie Everitt
Library of Congress Catalog Card Number: 92-93570
ISBN 0-8034-8962-5
All rights reserved.
All the characters in this book are fictitious,
and any resemblance to actual persons,
living or dead, is purely coincidental.

PRINTED IN THE UNITED STATES OF AMERICA
ON ACID-FREE PAPER
BY HADDON CRAFTSMEN, SCRANTON, PENNSYLVANIA

*Somewhere Near Paradise*

## Chapter One

"Get your hands off of it, you twerp!" It was a shrill command, in a tone and crackling timbre that Marcie recognized instantly. She couldn't see the owner of the voice, but it was a thirteen-going-on-fourteen voice; she knew that very well.

"You always get things your way!" This was a whine, at a pitch as familiar as the first—slightly younger, she'd judge.

Marcie rounded the copse of trees that crowded with their roots gnarling down the slope toward the water. Now she could see them: two boys, at the end of a boat dock. Push, shove, grapple, curse. The words that twelve- and thirteen-year-old boys—and girls too—used didn't surprise her anymore. Not after four years of teaching that age group. Or trying to.

"Stupid—little—nerd—" the larger of the two panted, struggling for the basis of the dispute, which seemed to be a fishing rod. Marcie leaned against a tree to watch. They'd sort it out soon enough, probably, though boys of any age were just no good at logical discussion, diplomacy, negotiations—

The smaller boy was knocked off his feet by a particularly vicious left jab. Marcie stood up straight, frowning. *Chill out,* she told herself. *They'll settle it between themselves* . . . but she could feel the idea of a peaceful late-afternoon stroll beside the lake simply evaporating. The bigger boy was just too much bigger.

It didn't seem fair. Marcie liked things fair.

The smaller boy had a nosebleed and was struggling against tears. "Think you're so big," he said a little weakly, swiping blood across his face and stepping back.

"Runny-nosed baby," the big boy said.

"Pig doodoo," the smaller one managed.

The bigger boy shoved. The small one fell.

Marcie whistled. Marcie's between-the-teeth whistles had stopped incipient playground riots on more than one occasion and caused a decided ringing in the ears for anyone who had the misfortune to be standing near her when her whistle split the atmosphere.

"*Knock it off, you two!*" she commanded as their startled faces turned toward her. They were surprised enough to step apart momentarily, anyway. She took two more steps forward. "Cool it," she said, "before one of you really gets hurt."

Apparently they didn't think she had the weight or the right to stop them. They were back at it before she'd even finished the sentence. That sort of thing had happened to her many times before, since she considered it her decided misfortune to be quite small and look ridiculously young.

But she'd also had some training in the martial arts— not a bad idea, if one had to teach in her part of Chicago. The knowledge that teach had a brown belt in judo was the psychological equivalent of carrying a big stick.

She started forward onto the dock. One way or another, she'd separate these two.

The water at the end of the dock suddenly erupted upward in a veritable geyser of golden drops—a geyser that roared.

In the center of the geyser was the source of the upheaval and the roar: a man. Marcie's eyes widened. A warlike Neptune rising naked right up out of the deeps, she thought—though, of course, the water there wasn't that deep, and he wasn't really naked, either, after all. Though that wasn't much of a suit he was wearing—and where in the heck had he come from, anyway?

His sudden appearance had shocked the boys as much as it had surprised her. She took a step backward, and the boys looked both scared and guilty.

Neptune pulled himself out onto the end of the dock with strong bronzed arms, looked at the boys, and then at Marcie.

"Okay," he growled. Marcie didn't know "okay" could sound so intimidating. Of course, coming from a man who was over six feet tall. . . . "Okay," he repeated, grabbing a boy by the nape of the neck with each hand. Each gigantic hand. "You two have been told before—don't come out here looking for trouble, or you're going to find it. Bringing a girlfriend with you isn't very smart, either."

Marcie blinked, doubting her hearing. Did he mean *her?* She opened her mouth to protest, but the giant was roaring on.

"You've been thieving rods from the boathouse again, looks like." He looked down at the disputed fishing rod. "Seems to me you two just might need your numskulls cracked together!"

"Now, wait just a minute," Marcie finally managed to say. Something in her tone and her bearing seemed to get through to the man at last, and he did a classic double take. He was just like the boys, unable to discuss things logically, negotiate, or use diplomacy. And she was very much afraid that he really *was* going to crack the boys' heads together. "That," she said firmly with her chin raised, "is no way to handle the situation."

"Now is that right?" He was looking at her even more closely, so closely that it made Marcie slightly nervous. "And just who are you, and what makes you think this is any of your darned business?"

"I'm Marcella Newberry, and 'my business' is working with kids. I teach in Chicago." She tried drawing herself up to her full height, but she was painfully aware that she was at least a foot shorter than he was, and that made it hard to look down her nose at him. She did her best.

"I don't think force should be used to settle disputes," she said a little stiffly. "Yours or theirs."

Good grief, the man reminded her of a bear. A golden bear, with close-cropped and dripping curly blond hair—both on his head and his jaw. She wasn't terribly fond of beards, no matter how well trimmed. And even his chest was furry. An excess of testosterone, she decided. He probably got that scar on the side of his forehead in some barroom brawl.

He was staring at her, rather insolently, she thought, from head to toe—as if she were the one wearing an itty-bitty Speedo and nothing else. "Stop that," she commanded, not sure whether she was talking about his treatment of the boys or his stare. Both probably.

Surprisingly, his grip relaxed. "Talking won't cut it where Kenny MacIntyre's concerned," he said. The bigger of the boys—presumably Kenny MacIntyre—

said something under his breath and sidled sideways. The other, eyeing the situation critically, followed suit.

"You don't have to crack skulls, anyway," Marcie said, at the same time that the man took a step forward and said, "This really *isn't* any of your business, you know."

The boys took advantage of the diversion to streak forward off the dock, brushing past Marcie as if she weren't even there. They were one hundred feet up the path before either of the adults reacted.

The bear shook his head, as if to clear water out of his ears, and let his hands fall to his sides. "You distracted me," he said accusingly. "And now they got away with it, didn't they?"

"Not entirely." Marcie felt a little defensive—and, she admitted inwardly, a little distracted herself. She found her voice with difficulty and pointed down at the fishing rod. "They left that behind, after all. Maybe they learned something."

"Now, I doubt that, darlin'. Kenny has his own brand of summer school—learning from the older tough kids who come out from the city in the summer. He thinks they're cool. He thinks graffiti is cool. He thinks being a bully is cool. He thinks cutting school is cool. He's hell-bent on going for a graduate degree in tough cool."

She could readily understand that particular problem—Marcie knew too well the kinds of kids he was learning from. But this man certainly didn't have the right approach to settling things, and she found her jaw tensing.

And was that a Texas accent? She didn't much like being called "darlin'" by a complete stranger, though there were certain things you could almost forgive Texans for. They couldn't he'p being different . . . a waterlogged Texas bear, rather than Neptune? Her curiosity was growing. "Where on earth did you come from, anyway?" she asked, frowning slightly at her own question. She wasn't sure if she were asking if he was from Texas, or if he was Neptune, or just what. She felt rattled, a feeling she rarely experienced and didn't like at all.

A hint of a smile lit the amber-brown eyes that looked back at her. Suddenly he didn't look nearly so intimidating. "You mean originally or just now?" he asked as if he'd been reading her mind. He picked up the fishing rod and examined it. "I swim along here every afternoon. Saw them come out of the boathouse. They've done it before—taken things."

"It's a difficult age," Marcie said thoughtfully. "Still. . . ." She looked away, closing her eyes momentarily. The way the sun sparked golden highlights off this man was unnerving and blinding. "It's your boathouse they're taking things from, then? And who *are* you?" She suddenly felt very tired. It had been a long day, driving out from Chicago, opening up the cottage, trying to get settled—and then dealing (again! still!) with nasty kids *and* a bear—

"It's my boathouse, and I'm Jim Wolverton." He gestured toward a painted sign that stood several feet to one side of the small dock with its neat boathouse. *Wolverton Boat Rentals,* it said. "And I still wish you'd kept your pretty little nose out of it." The hint of a smile was gone. "I'd rather have handled it myself."

She huffed. "*Honestly!*"

"Yup, honestly, it is a nice nose. And it's honestly my boathouse and my dock and my fishing rod, and it was my problem." An exaggerated—and phony—sigh made the muscles of his chest and shoulders tighten with tension and then relax. Marcie looked away quickly, wanting suddenly to leave and trying to figure out how to have a good, squelching, final exit line. "Teacher," he added, with just a hint of insolent teasing.

There was her opening. Not the best but certainly acceptable. "Seems to me somebody should teach *you* a few things about common courtesy," she said coldly and turned on her heel and walked briskly away from him.

He watched her go, unmoving. She reminded him of a dragonfly, darting off like that, quick and sure. Funny little thing—in those jeans and that bright shirt she really did look like a kid herself. A cute kid. Until you took a closer look, of course—then she didn't look like a kid at all.

Were dragonflies feisty? This one was. Not much substance there, but a lot of fast wing-flapping. Well, he couldn't blame her, in a way. He really hadn't been very gentlemanly . . . though she'd had no cause to go sticking her nose in what was basically his concern.

He shook himself and looked around for his towel— he'd left it here somewhere, hadn't he? Strange how he hadn't noticed until she'd left that there was a sudden coolness in the breeze.

Marcie took the long way back to the cottage, walking slowly and trying to soak in some of the peace she'd hoped to find when she'd set out. It was elusive.

But she did find a frog, a giant frog, on a rock in the laughing little creek that ran down to the lake. She stopped to stare, and he seemed not at all afraid of her, grinning his froggy grin and watching her with un-blinking eyes.

"Sam," she said. "You're Sam." Misty memories of childhood summers by the lake and a frog she'd named Sam swept over her. Some things didn't change, thank goodness. "I won't disturb you," she assured him. He blinked at last and flicked at a passing fly. "But do look out for wet bears, okay? Wet bears can be very disturbing." Sam disappeared into the brook with hardly a splash. Much more neatly than that Wolverton man would have done, she decided. He was just too much. In every way.

She found the dust in Gram's cottage exactly as she had left it when she'd started on her walk. But the cottage itself didn't seem the same without Gram. *Things are different now,* Marcie told herself. *The town is different; I'm different.* But she didn't want things to be different. She wanted to go back to the cocoon of childhood, and she couldn't.

She attacked the dust with Gram's old lamb's-wool duster, suddenly feeling a need for vigorous physical activity—something to take her mind off the peculiarly dazzling vision of Jim Wolverton surging up from the lake. *There are all kinds of water pollution,* she thought sourly, unable to banish the picture. She took the duster out onto the back porch to shake it and nearly fell over the cat.

She dropped the duster, grabbed the porch railing, and stared. A striped gray cat, it was, thin and wide-eyed, hunkering down to stare right back at her. "Nero?" Marcie asked. The cat's tail flicked—a slightly stubby tail. "Nero?"

Gram's cat had disappeared just about the time Gram died. But— "Nero." He stretched, eyed her warily, then came toward her with a raspy meow. "Oh, my. My goodness, Nero. We're going to have to feed you, aren't we, Nero? Feed you lots." She scooped him up and let herself in the door, the cat draped across her shoulders like an undernourished fur collar. She was sure she had a can of tuna. . . .

"Where on earth have you been?" she asked him, watching him inhale the tuna without lifting his head.

"Maybe not on earth at all. Who knows where cats go when they wander? Into some great, mythic catland, probably."

Marcie didn't breathe for a minute. The voice had come from behind her; she turned warily. A very substantial figure clad in what appeared to be a vintage muumuu stood just outside her screen door on the small back porch, filling it almost to overflowing.

"Sorry," the figure said in a rich contralto. "I didn't mean to startle you."

"I just didn't hear you come up—"

"I'm a quiet neighbor, dear. I'm Sarita Cox from next door, and I brought you some peanut-butter cookies. Nero is fond of peanut-butter cookies too. He finds that peanut-butter cookies have an effect almost like catnip."

It was a distinctly odd speech, but friendly. A tiny light of recollection flashed in the dim recesses of Marcie's subconscious. Gram had mentioned a rather unusual new neighbor—was it a couple of years ago? Wondering how Sarita Cox knew what Nero felt about peanut-butter cookies, she opened the door. Her visitor walked in—flowed in, would be more like it, in spite of her bulk—on tiny, silent, bare feet, putting a large covered platter on the table.

"Thank you. I adore peanut-butter cookies." Marcie

watched Nero twining himself gracefully around Sarita Cox's ankles, purring like a small turbine.

"Of course you do. I knew that." It was said matter-of-factly, as if Marcie's passion for cookies had been printed in the headlines of the *Chennowah Grove Gazette*. "I have an excellent memory and even better intuition. You look extremely young for your age; did you know that?"

Marcie knew that only too well. *"Bringing a girl-friend with you isn't very smart."* Marcie closed her eyes for a moment against the picture of Jim Wolverton dismissing her as a mere child, and she groped for words to answer Sarita Cox's strange, mixed statements.

"It really has been quite a day, hasn't it, dear?" Sarita's words jolted Marcie back to reality. "I won't stay now. You'll be here for quite a while, after all."

"For the summer, anyway," Marcie said. Any possibility of a logical train of thought had been derailed several sentences ago. The summer wasn't such a long time. . . . "I'll be going back to Chicago to teach once school starts, of course."

"Mmm . . . somehow I doubt that."

Marcie stared at her. Perhaps she was more tired than she thought; the conversation had all the elements of a dream.

Sarita grinned at her, gray eyes alive with humor and understanding. "You'll be busy, finding land for the social center," she explained kindly. "And, probably," she added, a faraway look in her eyes, "with a number of other things too. Yes, certainly with other things. Trust me."

It would be easy to trust Sarita Cox. Easier than trusting Jim Wolverton, who was, after all, an attrac-

tive man. And she'd had enough of attractive, untrust-
worthy men for quite a while.

And Sarita knew about Gram's bequest for a social
center. Well, the whole town probably did. But what
other things? She started to ask about that, but Sarita
cut her off. "Enjoy the cookies," she said. "And your
summer." In a whirl of multicolored muumuu, she
was gone as quietly as she had come.

Nero, apparently aware that Marcie was in a highly
befuddled state, took the opportunity to leap silently
and gracefully onto the kitchen table, eyes fixed on the
platter of cookies.

Marcie came back to earth with a thunk, feeling as
if she'd just been for a walk on the edge of a very thin
cloud. "Oh, no, you don't," she told him, scooping
the cookies up and putting them in the cupboard.

She found a bowl and poured milk for him and then
for herself. Plopping herself down in one of the old
pressed-back oak chairs, she lost herself in milk, one
carefully guarded cookie, and a cloud of preoccupation.

*She* wasn't the one who behaved strangely. It was
everybody else, making her feel a lot like Alice must
have felt when she met the white rabbit. First there'd
been that overbearing Wolverton man and then the
peculiar Sarita Cox.

But she *liked* Sarita Cox. Which was more than she
could say for Jim Wolverton; he had riled her so much
that she couldn't shake him from her mind.

Maybe she should have paid closer attention when
Gram had mentioned her next-door neighbor; she might
have been prepared for a certain amount of eccentricity.
But now . . . now it was too late. Gram was gone, after
a fall and a broken hip and then pneumonia, so quickly
that it had seemed like a bad dream.

Marcie hadn't been completely surprised by the fact that she had inherited the cottage near the lake. Gram had always said that it would be hers someday. But she was surprised—astonished would be more like it— at the size of what her grandmother had always referred to as her "nest egg," and Gram had set the cat among the pigeons with that codicil. Finding and purchasing the land, getting plans under way for construction. . . . Sarita was probably right; she'd have her hands full. Even small towns like Chennowah Grove had planning commissions and red tape.

She looked down at the hand that Sarita had held momentarily. Had she imagined a tiny current of deep understanding, almost like electricity, when Sarita had touched her? Ridiculous—or perhaps there was just electricity in the air. That might explain the tingle of tension she'd felt out there on the boat dock, talking to that awful man.

Marcie absently fed a piece of her cookie to Nero and nodded sagely to herself. That was it. There was probably a storm coming.

Jim Wolverton was a little later getting back to the restaurant than he'd planned. He'd toweled off roughly and then sat on the end of the dock, staring at the wooded shoreline opposite, until the westering sun glared ferociously into his eyes and reminded him that he had business to attend to. He wasn't, after all, just one of those casual tourists or summer visitors who could wander around, sticking their noses into other people's business. . . .

That's what she must be—a summer visitor. He'd never heard of Marcella Newberry before, or any other Newberry, for that matter, around Chennowah Grove.

And he'd been here for more than two years now, and surely he would have noticed her. He gathered up his jeans and shirt from the bank and slid into them; he put the purloined fishing pole back in the boathouse and checked the doors. That lock needed replacing. He should know by now that a man had to keep anything even halfway valuable locked away these days. . . .

For a few minutes he stood leaning on the weathered planks of the boathouse. Did that ridiculous little lady think she could actually *reason* with the likes of Kenny MacIntyre? And a teacher too. Just showed how flawed today's educational system was.

He suddenly visualized again the sparks of indignation in her eyes and found himself grinning foolishly. He shook himself sternly and straightened up. *Okay, Jim, let's get back to work.*

Kind of cute little thing she was, though. Prickly, but kind of pretty—something like a flowering cactus, maybe. Nice to look at but keep your hands off— though if she planned on spending the summer, he might like to find out if she were as prickly as she seemed.

*I said get back to work,* he reminded himself severely. He hadn't done much more than just look at any woman—with appreciation sometimes, but from a distance—ever since Sandy had died. Sandy— An explosion of four-year-old memory he'd thought was fading flashed blindingly inside his head. Sandy, her eyes wide with fear and desperation, grabbing the steering wheel, the guard rails and retaining wall seeming to race toward the oncoming car. Screams echoing down the corridors of his mind, and then nothing, nothing at all, until he woke up in the unquiet silence of a hospital room, full of pain and remorse. And Sandy was dead.

His hand strayed to the scar on his forehead, and he rubbed at it furiously, as if he could rub away the horror of the memory. He took a deep breath and stared out at the changing pattern of light on the waters while the nightmarish pictures faded. He'd made up his mind to go it alone after the accident . . . the only decision to make, obviously. Sure as hell, the right decision.

But—things changed. Maybe his unexpected appreciation of a prickly pear was actually a good sign. He'd have to think about that when he had the time. He picked up his bike and pedaled with unnecessary vigor back to the restaurant, trying to leave unresolved problems behind him.

"Hey, Jim, where you been? Joe's been having a fit—there's something wrong with the wiring to the ovens, and you've had three calls from Superior Steaks. Genna called and said she won't be in this evening, so I called Lois to fill in for her—all right? But then I won't have anyone to help bartend."

His assistant manager was on the verge of panic. Jim found himself, gratefully, caught up in immediate, solvable problems.

"Now, Chet," he said soothingly. "Lois will do fine, and Superior Steaks can wait until tomorrow. I'll fill in with you behind the bar. I don't suppose you checked the circuit breakers?"

Chet looked crestfallen. The power problems had occurred before, but Chet's acquaintance with electrical gadgets seemed to be confined to plugging in his stereo. And Joe Bender, the chef, wasn't much better.

Jim took care of it. He'd have to check out the whole

wiring system one of these days, he supposed. Good thing he had a background in construction; he'd done a lot to the old lakeside café since taking it over, and he was proud of it, but there was always more to be done.

For the next hour he was busy enough to push any thoughts of that afternoon encounter far from his mind. He didn't even have time to don cowboy boots and a Stetson, part of his usual costume for greeting his guests.

But a large party of summer people came in around seven-thirty, and he found he was scanning them from behind the bar for a small, bright-eyed lady with a certain tilt to her chin.

"Chet," he said, as offhandedly as he could manage, "there aren't any Newberrys in town, are there? Ran into one today, couldn't quite place the name."

The bar was busy, and Chet was hectically stacking glasses behind the bar. He paused a minute, then grinned at Jim. "Well, now, yes, sort of," he said ambiguously. "She always was a pretty thing. Her folks lived in Chicago, but she used to spend her summers here. Had all the boys in town jealous of each other all summer, she did, when we were kids."

"Who?" Jim asked, knowing darned well who.

"Marcie Newberry. Granddaughter of Anita Colburn. Mrs. Colburn owned that little house at the end of Shore Drive and died just this spring. I guess Marcie inherited the house, and rumor has it that there was some kind of provision for a town social center. Heard she was coming to spend the summer to straighten it all out."

"Oh." Jim swiped ineffectually at the bar. "Too

bad.'' It sounded odd, so he added, ''That she died, I mean. I guess I didn't know her.''

''I doubt it. She kept herself to herself.'' Chet was still grinning. ''But from the expression on your face, I think you've met Marcie. Good luck. You'll need it.''

Jim tried to think of a good squelching remark but couldn't come up with one. A blowsy blonde at the end of the bar resolved his problem for him. ''Hey, you guys ever heard the word 'service'? Gonna stand there yakking all night?''

Jim drew himself up to his full height and managed to stroll toward her like a genuine cowboy, even without the aid of his Stetson and boots. He assured her, turning on the full force of his smile, that he did indeed know the word service, and just what kind was she looking for?

She melted.

Marcie sat at the kitchen table in the dimming light of early evening, happily surrounded by her lists. And by her sublists.

So many things to do, and she always felt better when she had everything down in an orderly fashion—the bank, the attorney, the real estate office, shopping for a new swimsuit. . . . She glowed at her lists.

And maybe, once she had her new swimsuit, she could think about going for a swim. Tomorrow afternoon would be good, at about the same time that she'd gone out today. She actually had pen in hand, about to add that item to her list, when she stopped herself. Just exactly what was her subconscious doing to her, anyway? Her subconscious answered by presenting her with a brilliant picture of a broad-shouldered man arising from the water, and she caught her breath. *He* was not on any of her lists, nor would he be. Supercilious and arrogant, condescending, treating her like a child and calling her "darlin'"—accusing her of interfering in something that was his business.

The old-fashioned doorbell jangled and startled her out of her contemplation of lists. The voice that floated through to her from the front of the house made a small, warm glow take the place of the admiration; it had to be Ellen. She'd recognize Ellen's soft voice in the wilds of Tibet.

"Marcie? You here? I saw your car out there. Can I come in?"

Marcie flew through the house to unlatch the screen door, lists forgotten. There was a flurry of hugs and half-completed sentences. Ellen Cunningham had been her best summer friend for as long as she could remember, though they hadn't seen much of each other for the past few years.

"You look great," Ellen told her, pushing her away at last and studying her critically. "No older at all—as usual. Will you be here all summer? Aren't you married yet? Can you still whistle through your teeth? Did you know Nero was sitting on your front porch with a friend?"

Marcie laughed. "Whoa. Come on through to the kitchen. I made some lemonade, and I have cookies, and we can— Did you say Nero has a friend on the front porch?" She craned her neck and looked out the door, switching on the porch light.

Nero sat, looking vastly satisfied, beside a slender, well-marked calico. "Well," Marcie said. "I see. I think. Nero?"

Nero *prr-owed* at her, and the calico managed to look hungry.

"More cat food, I think," Marcie said consideringly, taking one last look at the pair of cats before she ushered Ellen toward the back of the house. Summer romances blossoming all over the world. Foolish creatures, to be so taken in. "Not expecting, I hope," she muttered toward the calico, trying to exorcise the little twinge of self-pity that had tweaked at her heart in spite of herself.

"Not *me*," Ellen said innocently. "Not even engaged. In anything interesting, anyway. How about you?"

She sidestepped that one with a negative wave of the hand.

But it occurred to her that if anyone could tell her who Jim Wolverton was, it would be Ellen. Ellen always knew exactly what was going on; she could probably tell Marcie the man's entire life history, if Marcie wanted to hear it. Which she didn't. She just wanted confirmation that the man was a lout and a boor, though she wished she could quit seeing that insidious vision of the sun striking golden sparks off that blond head.

Again she sidestepped. Ellen might misunderstand if she brought him into the conversation too quickly. So she led the conversation rapidly through a variety of other important issues, such as who had married whom recently, the difficult task she was going to have finding land this summer, and affirming that she could, indeed, still whistle through her teeth. She wondered fleetingly what kind of an impression her piercing whistle had made on Jim Wolverton. It never failed to make *some* kind of an impression. She hoped it had made his ears ring.

"And who," she asked offhandedly at last, "is running the boat rentals these days? Someone new in town, I take it."

"Oh, Marcie, lucky you! You've met him already!"

"I've been in town two hours, and I've already had a fight with a large, rude creature with a beard—if you call that lucky."

"For heaven's sake, why would you want to fight with *him?* Every other woman in town under seventy wants to cuddle him. At least. Jim moved here two years ago. Just liked the town, he said. He came from somewhere in Texas, but no one knows a lot about what he did before he got to Chennowah Grove. You'll love him once you get to know him."

"I doubt that." She let the question about why she was fighting with him go. Thinking about the whole scene out there on the dock still made the hairs on the back of her neck rise alarmingly; she must have been even angrier than she'd thought at the time. And there were so many other things to talk about that were more important, after all. . . .

". . . and Buzz Maddox is the editor of the *Grove Gazette* now—did you know that?" Ellen was saying. "His father was very sick last year and decided to semiretire, so Buzz took over. I kind of run the office for him." A faint peachy glow on Ellen's cheeks betrayed her, but Marcie didn't let on. She'd always suspected that Ellen had worshiped Buzz since junior high, though Ellen never came right out and said so. Marcie had always thought it would be better if she had; she suspected Buzz returned Ellen's feelings but was too in awe of Ellen's straight-A average, her popularity, and her bright efficiency to say so.

"I think he still has his old crush on you, Marcie," Ellen said with only a touch of sadness.

"Oh, I'm sure he doesn't," Marcie said briskly. "We were always just good friends, you know." Buzz, with his long legs and red hair, had always reminded her of a half-grown setter pup—a creature not to be taken too seriously. It was hard to imagine him grown up and editing the local weekly newspaper. It might be a good idea to change the subject, though a small voice was asking her if she might just play Cupid this summer.

Ridiculous. Play Cupid when she couldn't even begin to handle her own loves and emotions!

But Ellen was still full of questions and plans. She'd even brought the latest copy of the *Gazette,* with promising real estate ads circled in red.

"Your grandmother's plans are so marvelous for Chennowah Grove, Marcie," she said. "Since the high school closed two years ago and the kids are being bused to Dunwoodie County High, we really feel the pinch. No auditorium. No volleyball field. Seniors' Bingo Night is spilling out of the church basement and right off into the cemetery. Little theater has become so little it's invisible. Your gram was just wonderful. . . ."

"She was," Marcie said with a catch in her throat. "But I only hope I can handle all this." She hadn't been very skilled at dealing with problems over the past year—with romance, or school superintendents, or even roaring wet giants.

"You!" Ellen laughed. "You can handle anything, Marcie—you always could." And then she was asking how Marcie liked teaching and whether she had anyone special in her life—as if she were seeing into her thoughts.

And the answers, if she was honest, were so negative—a hardheaded principal, difficult kids, and parents who were worse, budget cuts, a possible school closure, an uncertain future—and a broken engagement. Semi-engagement, anyway.

The last fact she added quickly, as if to slide it into the conversation unnoticed. The year's problems—and Michael was the most hurtful of them—had left quite a few random bruises on her psyche. Michael and his cheating and his vague promises about a life together that he hadn't meant at all. . . . But Ellen was the noticing type and didn't let Marcie get away with sneaking mousily around the subject. And maybe it was a good thing to tell the nonjudgmental Ellen about it.

"I was a stupid fool, and I got burned. But that's all in the past," she concluded, sitting ramrod straight in her chair and glaring at the calendar on the wall as if the whole thing had been its fault. "I won't make the same mistake twice."

Ellen commiserated. "I'm sure you won't, Marcie. Anyone can make a mistake. And you have the summer here to recuperate, and there's so much to do. Look, Buzz and I want to take you out to dinner. Someplace special." She had a funny little grin on her face that Marcie couldn't quite figure out. "The old Chennowah Café has been completely redone. It's called Gentleman Jim's now—wonderful food. You'll just love it. I guarantee it." She reached for her small handbag and her car keys, looking smug.

"What are you hatching?" Marcie asked suspiciously.

"Me? Hatching? No way. Just set your taste buds for a fabulous Texas barbecue. Best thing on Jim Wolverton's menu." She gave Marcie a peck on the cheek and was gone, letting in a pair of very sneaky felines before the front door slammed shut.

Marcie stood speechless in the middle of the floor. "*Jim Wolverton's* menu?" she finally managed to squeak, but Ellen was long gone. It was a conspiracy. A plot. She wouldn't go. Yes, she would. He couldn't intimidate *her*. And now which of the two of them, she or Ellen, was the one who was going to try playing Cupid this summer?

She stomped her foot in exasperation and made herself sit down and eat two more peanut-butter cookies in an attempt to clear her mind. They didn't help much.

## Chapter Two

It was late before Marcie trailed wearily up the narrow stairs toward the welcome idea of a shower and bed. Feeling slightly guilty, she put the cats out—and added "litter box" to her list. There was a cricket-chirp quietness to the night. She should sleep well, after such a chaotic jumble of a day.

Still, she lay there for quite a while, almost wishing the increasingly noisy crickets and the tree frogs would hush up and leave her alone with her thoughts, although her thoughts weren't all pleasant. She had come back to what she thought was the paradise of her childhood, only to find that the golden gates were tarnished and that some of the angels seemed to have lost their wings. And she'd never heard of an angel with a Texas accent, so obviously he was in the wrong place.

Her thoughts gradually trailed off into swirling dream pictures—pictures that were fanciful variations of the day's events.

It was around three that she was abruptly awakened, snatching at the edges of a disintegrating dream of a frog, a rather handsome (but overly furry) bear, and two cats—with fishing poles—feasting on a Texas barbecue at the end of a boat dock.

There had been a piercing noise— She mumbled

and turned over, half listening, wanting to go back and join the dream picnic. She was sure the bear was about to say or do something terribly important, and she didn't want to miss it.

But that had been a scream. She hauled herself reluctantly out of bed and padded across the floor to pull back the light floral curtains. A star-spattered night, peaceful—a night for romance, not screams. No lights came on in the other houses. No dogs barked. Had it been part of her dreams? She didn't think so.

A light went off in the old Eddleston house built proudly back in the hilly meadows behind Gram's cottage over one hundred years ago. A few minutes later a car with only parking lights slipped down the drive and quietly disappeared.

Maybe the noise was one of the cats, but if so, she'd have to have a serious talk with them. She still didn't feel at ease. She pulled the old Adirondack rocker up to the window and sat staring out for many minutes, sleep as far away as the stars. Probably as the result of that dream she'd been having, she found herself thinking about Jim Wolverton.

In the middle of the night like this, completely alone, she could guiltily admit to herself that there was something very attractive about the man, high testosterone level and all—physically, at least. Come to think of it, his—animal magnetism, that was the right term—could probably be attributed to that very fact of a high testosterone level.

She wondered if all that fur could be as bristly as it looked. Maybe it was as soft as teddy-bear fur.

Mentally she reached out to the vivid image in her mind, running light, inquiring fingertips from jaw to shoulders to chest. . . . She tugged her wandering,

WATERLOO HIGH SCHOOL LIBRARY
1464 INDUSTRY RD.
ATWATER, OHIO 44201

unsettling thoughts back into order and pushed the disturbingly realistic pictures from her mind. There was probably a Mrs. Bear, after all—and three little bears. But no, there wasn't. What Ellen had said about his being a mystery man with all the women in town half in love with him made him sound distressingly single. Not that it mattered. He was far too bearish and heavy-handed to appeal to her in a cool, intelligent, rational way.

And from here on she was going to be cool, intelligent, and rational. No more Michaels.

*Put it from your mind, Marcella*. There was so much to be done this summer, and she was supposed to be helping her heart to heal, not finding new ways to fracture it. She finally got up and found a pad of scratch paper and a pencil in one of the drawers of the nightstand and worked on her lists. The darkness was giving way to a rosy glow in the east before she was able to drift off again into a fitful sleep.

With the consequence, of course, that she awoke with a head full of fog and forgetfulness, and it was nearly noon before she donned denim skirt, camp shirt, and sandals, and drove her little Honda down to the town square to begin her errands.

Naturally, everything took longer than she thought it would. She'd almost forgotten about the leisurely pace of a small town, and she ran into people she hadn't seen for so long . . . but at last there was just one more stop at Milburn's Hardware on First Street for a new window fan and light bulbs, and she'd be almost done.

Stowing the bulky boxed fan onto the backseat of her small car—which was already loaded with other purchases—turned out to be more difficult than she thought. Why, oh, why, did these manufacturers have to pack everything into such unforgiving boxes? She plunked the carton down on the sidewalk and stood back to glare at the whole situation.

"Now, that just doesn't seem fair, a little thing like you having to load that up all by yourself. Why didn't Bob Milburn send one of the boys out to do that for you? Here, let me help you." The slight drawl and the word that did sound quite a bit like "he'p" made her close her eyes and take a deep breath before she turned.

He was alarmingly close to her, but only for a moment. Then he was stepping around her, reaching into the car to move bags, slipping the oversized box in as easily as if it had been a copy of the *Grove Gazette.*

Marcie struggled for the right words. "Thank you" would probably be appropriate, but her first reaction was to tell him that, actually, she could have done it herself. Little thing like you, indeed!

She settled for saying nothing for the moment, just watching as he bent to the task—nice view, she admitted reluctantly. Very nice. His jeans were snug and trim and covered considerably more than that minimal bathing suit had yesterday.

*Cool it, Marcie,* a small warning voice told her, but it was a *very* small voice, and she nearly didn't hear it.

"There," he said, straightening and turning to look down at her with a grin.

Well, darn, he hadn't realized it was so *far* down until he got this close to her. He felt his grin waver and fade. She was looking up at him with the oddest expression in her eyes—dark-blue unreadable eyes, under that short shock of soft dark hair.

"Thank you very much, Mr. Wolverton." Stiffly, as if it were nearly impossible to force the words out.

"My pleasure. And my name's Jim."

She continued to look up at him with that same darned expression, only now there was a hint of a frown pulling her eyebrows together, and the blue of her eyes had turned to midnight. And she didn't say a thing. It was unheard of for him to be at a loss for words around a pretty woman, but—

"I think maybe I owe you an apology, little lady," he heard himself saying. He hadn't intended to say anything of the sort. "For thinking you were one of the kids yesterday, I mean. I was angry at them and probably sounded pretty darned rude."

"Yes, Mr. Wolverton, you did. However, your apology is accepted." She didn't add "grudgingly," but that's what it sounded like. It also seemed as if she were deliberately trying to sound like a schoolmarm.

"My name's still Jim."

"I didn't think you'd changed it."

If he wasn't misreading her, there were the beginnings of a smile in her eyes now. And then the corners of her mouth quirked up, or at least one corner did, into a charming little crooked smile, lips slightly parted.

He forced himself to look away, down at the roll of electrical wire he'd put on the sidewalk when he'd yielded to the misguided impulse to help this— The word cactus came back to him again. He picked up the wire; intelligent reasoning began to work its way back into his conscious mind. Where did she get off, using that superior schoolteacher approach with him, anyway, when all he was trying to do was help—and apologize?

"Don't tell me you're still put out about the way I

handled Kenny MacIntyre, *Miss* Newberry,'' he rasped. ''If you knew more about him, you'd understand.''

''Maybe you can explain it to me. Someday.'' Her voice was full of phony honey, and her smile had disappeared.

''Maybe I could, if you were of a mind to listen.''

She rounded the corner of the small blue car as if she were running away from him, but stopped before opening the driver's side door. ''I really don't like bullies who pick on people smaller than they are,'' she stated flatly and slid into the car.

Now, just a darned minute! Was she talking about Kenny MacIntyre—or him?

He bent to look through the car at her and reined in the impulse to continue the argument. If that's what it was. ''It would be a good idea for you to fasten your seat belt, Miss Newberry,'' he said, proud of his cool rationality.

''It would be a good idea if you'd mind your own business, Mr. Wolverton,'' she returned, echoing his tone too exactly, putting the car in gear while ignoring his helpful suggestion.

''Hey, wait!'' he yelled at the rear bumper of the car, but it was too late. She wasn't actually burning rubber, but the front end of the car was decidedly higher than the rear, and all of it was pulling away like a scalded jackrabbit.

He watched her go, his jaw clenched with exasperation. All he'd tried to do was apologize, after all. Maybe he shouldn't have told her to fasten her seat belt, though he was just trying to be helpful. Ever since the accident, he'd had this insecure feeling about women and cars . . . she shouldn't be driving like that.

Try to be nice to some people, and all you got in return was a kick in the teeth—though in her case, or in his case, or whatever the case might be, that would have to be some kick.

The exasperation disappeared. He smiled a little and turned away, unconsciously rubbing the scar on his forehead with his free hand.

Let her go. Women! His daddy had always told him that they were completely unpredictable, and his daddy should have known, having been married three times before his untimely death in a freak skydiving accident. He strode back to his truck, determined to put Marcella Newberry out of his mind once and for all.

Marcie slowed down once she'd turned the corner onto Elm Street. One simply didn't drive the streets of Chennowah Grove as if they were the Eisenhower Expressway.

"Little thing like you"—"Little lady"—condescension!

Her stomach was tied in knots; her hands clenched on the steering wheel. She coasted to a stop near the curb, fastened her mutely reproachful seat belt, and leaned her head back against the headrest, breathing deeply.

*Marcie, you're overreacting,* she told herself. She knew what she was doing: She was being overly defensive, a result of spending a good part of her adult life trying to convince people that she wasn't as young and inexperienced as she looked.

But there was more to it than that. There was a wariness too, because Jim Wolverton really was so darned attractive. *Handsome is as handsome does,* she reminded herself in Gram's tone of voice. The man

acted so darned sure of himself and in control and so—
so—*big*.

*He was just trying to be helpful, Marcie. Be fair.
You like things fair.*

But. . . .

*You mustn't let little things upset you like that.*

But . . . and, anyway, he's not little.

The small voice in her mind laughed at her. "Forget
it!" she said sharply out loud.

She had so many other things to think about, after
all.

There was one more item on the list she'd carefully
taped to her dashboard: Stop by Chennowah Properties
and see what kind of real estate might be on the market
this summer. That was, after all, one of her main reasons for being in Chennowah Grove, wasn't it?

Two hours later Marcie sat on her back-porch steps
and frowned, absently scratching a purring Nero behind
his pointy ears. She'd almost memorized the lists of
available property, and there wasn't much that was
suitable, unless she wanted to build the activities center
in the middle of a marsh behind the city dump.

She really had thought that she could get things well
under way over the summer months, but it appeared
likely that she'd hardly get started. There was just so
much to do that she felt overwhelmed. If she found
the land, where would she find a contractor? And how
long would it take to close the deal? And—

Come fall, she'd be driving back and forth between
the city and Chennowah Grove every weekend. She
wasn't sure she liked that idea, not one bit—even
though she loved Chennowah Grove.

It was hot and sticky, and her furry purring lap robe
wasn't helping. A bit crossly, she removed Nero from

her lap and stood up and stretched. Nero stalked off huffily to join Patches in the shadows under the porch.

Now, she decided, might be a good time to go for a swim; in the evening, when it was cooler, she could take a drive to look at the few sites that looked possible, if not probable.

A few minutes later, feeling downright resplendent in the brashly bright new suit, an oversized white shirt, and floppy sandals, she made her way down the path toward the lake. One short detour to look for Sam—but Sam wasn't there. Of course she couldn't expect him to be sitting in the same spot at the same time every afternoon, but still she felt disappointed. A frog on a rock was one thing about Chennowah Grove that hadn't seemed to change at all.

And, of course, they wouldn't serve frogs' legs at Gentleman Jim's, would they? Would *he?* Now, that was an absolutely uncalled-for, ridiculous thought. What had brought it to her mind, anyway?

The slant of the sun through the leaves gave her the answer. This was the time she'd been here yesterday, and look what had happened.

But she had a right to be here. Besides, she'd just about made up her mind to mellow out where Jim Wolverton was concerned. She'd be objective—and cool—and distantly polite. The decision made her feel marvelously virtuous—partly because she knew that being objective and cool and distant with Jim Wolverton would be a Personal Challenge. But she could handle that.

She almost skipped down the slippery path toward the lake, slipped out of shirt and sandals, and waded through the shallows to the deeper waters. The lake welcomed her with cool, caressing wavelets, and she felt the tensions draining away.

Wonderful—there was no one around. No one at all.

On the shore beyond the copse of trees, beyond the dock, Jim Wolverton stood partially hidden behind a stand of shore willow. He watched, unmoving.

Twenty yards offshore, the lithe, shapely figure in the brilliant suit dived, surfaced, played in the water like a seal . . . but no seal ever looked like that. If he'd seen her like that yesterday, he'd never have mistaken her for a child. Never.

She waded in toward shore, and he stepped back into deeper concealment, feeling foolishly like a Peeping Tom. That curve of throat, the soft curves of her figure—no child, this.

She sat down on the beach and then stretched for one long languorous moment, then, closing her eyes, tilted her head toward the sun, letting the straps of her suit slip a little way down her arms.

He closed his own eyes, seeking to seal that beautiful picture—like a snapshot—within his memory. She was a woman, a beautiful woman. He opened his eyes to verify that fact once again.

For a moment he considered sneaking away. But that would be cowardly.

He could still see that funny little crooked half smile she had given him that morning. There was something earnestly gamine, infinitely appealing about her, and he didn't quite know how to handle that.

He wanted desperately to protect her—from what, he didn't know—and she obviously didn't want protecting.

And he felt instinctively that he'd better not sneak up on her. She looked blissful about being alone, and his very presence seemed to set up negative vibrations. Very deliberately, he crashed through the underbrush like a spooked mustang and splashed noisily out into the water. When he sneaked a look sideways toward Marcie, she'd pulled her straps up where they belonged and was sitting motionless, looking apprehensively in his direction.

Marcie swallowed hard. All that noise had to be either a large, badly misplaced amphibious Army maneuver or her Personal Challenge. And how long had he been standing on the shore? Her arm snaked out and grabbed the white shirt, pulling it on quickly over her suit. *Since when are you so modest?* she asked herself wryly, watching Jim Wolverton pull himself up on his elbows out at the end of the dock.

"Good afternoon," he said, as if they met like this all the time. "Nice day for a swim. The water feels great."

The man was a reassuring barrel of platitudes, and he wasn't coming any closer; he perched at the end of the dock, leaving space between them. She relaxed. "I know. I've already had my swim. As a matter of fact, I was just leaving." But she didn't move.

"Well, now, that's a shame. We could have swum together. You know, you really shouldn't come out here all alone like this. It's a good idea to swim with a buddy."

There he went again, telling her what to do. "Why?" she asked sweetly. "Are there sharks in Lake Chennowah these days? And where is *your* buddy?"

"Oh—well. I'm a strong swimmer."

"So am I. And I don't make nearly as much noise

at it as you seem to do, either.'' She stood up and slipped her feet into her sandals. It was time to go back to the cottage. Her Personal Challenge was being insulting again, sitting there on the end of the dock as if he owned it and Chennowah Grove as well. Darn him!

''Don't rush off. I thought we might have a talk.''

In spite of herself, she took a few steps out on the dock, staring at him suspiciously. ''About what?'' she asked, once again aware of how the rays of sunlight glimmered about him, making him look like some fabled Viking or a golden sea god arising from his watery kingdom.

''Maybe about Kenny MacIntyre?'' he suggested hopefully. ''Why don't you come out and sit on the end of the dock, and I can tell you why I was so upset with him yesterday?''

''Why don't you come up here?'' she countered. ''We can sit in the shade, at least, if we're going to have another argument.''

He seemed to growl at that idea, but she couldn't make out what he was saying. She barely made out the words ''discuss, not argue,'' and then he shook his head. ''Maybe this isn't a good time for it,'' he said. ''Maybe some other time.'' He paused, looking at her so intently that she instinctively backed away a step. ''You do look very pretty today,'' he said and slipped away from the dock, sidestroking quietly parallel to the shore and still watching her with that unnerving intensity.

''Maybe,'' she agreed, answering his first observation and ignoring his second. ''I do have things to do at the cottage. Nice seeing you, anyway.'' It really wasn't quite a lie. ''Enjoy your swim,'' she flung over her shoulder at him, forcing her feet away from the beach and up the path. Enough of this. There were things on her lists that needed to be taken care of.

The impish voice in her mind that often raised unwelcome questions was prodding at her again—asking how long Jim Wolverton had been there before she actually saw him. Had he been watching her? Creepy thought. She told the voice to be quiet.

Odd how there was a feeling of warmth between her shoulder blades. He was watching her walk away—probably still leering.

She didn't look back.

"*That's* the old Chennowah Café?" Marcie asked incredulously.

"Nope, that's Gentleman Jim's," Buzz Maddox said, easing the car into an empty slot in the almost-full parking lot.

Obviously it was; it said so in big gothic letters, black on a cleverly weathered white, across the front. Almost like a movie set, Marcie thought. Well, a "B" movie, maybe.

Ellen and Buzz had picked her up at seven, and they'd driven through town the long way—talking about the growth and changes in the town, the changes in housing values.

The latter she'd seen for herself. Property was high—and beginning to get scarce. Chennowah Grove was changing, though lake and town had retained a quaint charm in spite of the incursions of retirees, summer people—and transplanted Texans.

Buzz and Ellen understood her feelings. They commiserated with her over real estate prices during the roundabout drive to the restaurant, made suggestions, and laughed together over small things; it seemed almost as if they were still very young—and yet, and yet. . . . She sat in the backseat by devious design, leaving Ellen to share the front with Buzz. He'd looked a little disappointed, this new-old Buzz who had grown up and filled out, his auburn hair tamed, his face now adult, but the look in his twinkling blue eyes was still the same.

He twinkled at her just a little too much, walking toward the broad veranda of Gentleman Jim's, Ellen on one arm and herself on the other. Marcie sighed inwardly and hoped Ellen wasn't suffering twinges of jealousy.

She'd worked hard to gear herself up for this evening. The prospect of seeing Jim Wolverton again had been . . . unsettling. She didn't know how to act toward him without overreacting; she'd made up her mind to be cool, tolerant, unflappable.

"What do you think of those windows?" Ellen was asking, and Marcie made herself concentrate on the question. Stained-glass windows glowed along the front, under the broad overhang of the veranda; there was even a hitching post.

"Looks sort of like—" she started and stopped abruptly. At the big swinging center doors stood a tall bearded man in a Stetson and boots, chatting amiably with arriving and departing guests. He looked a bit like the town marshal, she decided. He hadn't seen them approaching, and even as she watched, he disappeared inside momentarily.

*No doubt to crack some heads together,* Marcie thought, and smiled sweetly at the attractive hostess who ushered them to a table at the side of the small dance floor. There was an even smaller bandstand, though there was no band in evidence. The background music, however, was definitely country-and-western—which was to be expected, she supposed. There was no sign of the Gentleman himself, though. Marcie sighed with what she assured herself was relief.

She absorbed the decor, the music, the ambiance. A bit of Texas in the middle of northern Illinois—not bad, she had to admit. Not bad at all.

"The ribs," Ellen told Marcie. "Jim does wonderful things with ribs."

"Oh, does he?" The mental picture that Ellen's words brought to Marcie's mind had nothing to do with barbecue. But then, she had a tendency to be ticklish, anyway.

Buzz ordered for them with a casual panache that somehow touched her and made her feel strangely sad. Grown up, all of them. *Nothing remains static,* she reminded herself again, *but I just don't feel that much older. Most of the time, anyway.* She tried valiantly to keep track of the conversation through the selection, the ordering, the cocktails, but caught herself sneaking sideways glances toward the door, the bar, toward—

"Well, now, it's mighty nice to see you folks here tonight," the unexpected voice drawled behind her. She placed her Margarita very, very carefully on the blue-and-white checked tablecloth and straightened her shoulders. "Hi, Maddox. Good evenin', Ellen. Haven't seen you for a while, and don't you look pretty!"

Shouldn't he have said "howdy," if he were to stay in character? *Stop it, Marcie. . . .*

A large, strong hand with a hint of golden hair catching the light reached past her toward Buzz—Brian's—outstretched one. There was another hand just like it, she knew without looking, resting on the back of her chair. She didn't dare lean back. She just didn't move at all.

Buzz was introducing them while Ellen beamed; Marcie Newberry, Jim Wolverton— *"Why'd you come in here lookin' like that?"* came Dolly Parton's song over the loudspeaker, swirling through the chatter of guests.

"Oh, we've met," Jim said. "Casually, you might say. Although, from another standpoint, you might say I've seen quite a bit of her since she's been in town."

Marcie turned her head slowly to look up at the man standing behind her. She wasn't quite sure what to make of his tone of voice. Her new swimsuit wasn't *that* revealing.

There was a mischievous undercurrent in his voice that slipped up from between the words and teased feather-light along the sensitive trails of her consciousness. Was he trying to make it seem as if there were something between them? Already? And was that a hint of a leer?

She blushed. She couldn't help herself.

He read her blush correctly. Poor little thing was pretty sensitive. He almost felt sorry for her. "She was down at the dock the other day when Kenny MacIntyre pulled one of his tricks," he said smoothly. "We had what I reckon you might call a brief conversation."

"*You* might call it that. Actually, I think it was an argument." She sounded a little strained, he thought, but still ready to do battle. He quit feeling sorry for her.

"Just a slight difference of opinion. All right with you, Maddox, if I ask the little lady to dance for a few minutes before your dinner gets here?" There were a few couples on the dance floor now, and he could afford to take some time off from his hosting duties.

"I can speak for myself, you know," Marcie murmured sweetly. He was at it again with that "little lady" bit, but she'd promised herself to be tolerant and cool and—what was that other word?—oh, yes, unflappable. So far, she wasn't doing all that well.

Then she immediately surprised herself by adding that yes, she'd love to dance, and found herself on the dance floor, wondering just how anyone so big and heavy-handed in his attitudes could be so light on his feet.

And he was obviously trying to be nice, making no further reference to having seen a lot of her. And she certainly wasn't about to bring it up.

"You look mighty pretty tonight—you and Ellen both."

To her own annoyance, she was absurdly pleased by the compliment. She hadn't known whether to dress up or down for the occasion and had settled somewhere between with a silky-blue shirtwaist she particularly liked. And anything from western wear to designer dresses seemed to be in evidence here.

"Blue becomes you," he added.

Was there no end to this man's blarney? Or what did they call blarney in Texas? Then she remembered that the phrase had to do with bulls, and she smiled in spite of herself. "Goes with your eyes. You really have very pretty eyes, particularly when you're smiling." He really knew how to pile it on thick too.

"Thank you." She tried not to smile so much; she probably looked like a Cheshire cat. She was acutely aware of the feel of his hand on her back, leading her through the increasingly crowded floor with a light touch, and she felt her thought processes tangling. This wasn't so bad, after all. As a matter of fact, it was— well, she wouldn't define it. Eyes, that's what he was saying. Something about her eyes. She must say something sensible, something detached.

''And yours are—'' She stopped herself. Men didn't have pretty eyes—that wouldn't sound right. His were peculiarly probing—that's what they were, but she couldn't say that. They glowed, that deep amber-brown with hints of gold—almost like one of the cats, she thought. First he'd reminded her of a bear, now of a cat. That was it. That stubbornness and self-assurance—he must be a Leo.

''Mine are what?'' he asked, genuinely curious.

''Lionish.'' It sounded somewhat silly. ''What's your sign?''

''Neon.'' He said it without missing a beat and whisked her around energetically in response to a sudden change in the tempo of the music. Maybe it was some version of a Texas two-stomp, she thought breathlessly, chuckling a little. Whatever it was, it was fun—and a change of mood from the slow dancing. Which was probably for the best.

With a strange sense of relief, Jim saw the waiter wheeling the trolley toward her table. He'd welcomed that sudden change of pace in the music; he had found himself wanting to hold her closer and closer, and it left him with an unaccustomed sense of uncertainty. He often had a whirl around the dance floor with a customer—from little girls to elderly women. But it wasn't quite like this.

She fit in his arms so well. She was so complex— so tiny, so fragile in appearance, and so tough. She was devilishly sexy in that clingy blue dress that flared around excellent legs.

But he didn't want to get deeply involved with a woman. A turn around the dance floor was all right, but—

He led her back to the table, saying the polite, smooth things he could always find to say to attractive female customers, but his mind wasn't on them. One part of it was telling him to back off, and the other was telling him that, after all, it was only human for a healthy man to admire an appealing woman. He was human. He was healthy. She was certainly appealing. And, after all, it didn't mean he had to get branded and tied down for life, did it?

"Thank you, ma'am," he said, trailing one hand lightly across her shoulder. Even he could hear the slight huskiness in his voice, and he cleared his throat. "We'll have to do that again sometime. Real soon. Enjoy your dinner, folks."

He melted into the crowd in the busy restaurant with a slight swagger that Marcie watched with a thoughtful frown.

"I think you've made a conquest," Ellen whispered. Buzz just looked thoughtful, glancing from Ellen to Marcie.

"Why, darlin', that's just part of his stock in trade. He can't he'p flirting with his female customers," Marcie crooned with a touch of sarcasm. "He's probably in love with his horse." But there was a twinge of disappointment tugging at the edges of her ego. When they'd first gone out on the floor, she'd thought he actually meant his compliments. Then she'd sensed a sudden change, and she had no idea what had caused it.

Obviously her very first impression of him had been correct, and she'd been foolish to moon over his undeniable masculine attractions in the middle of the night. *Trust your first impressions, Marcie.* She would put that thought on one of her lists first thing tomorrow.

In the meantime, the barbecue really was fantastic, and the three of them had so much catching up to do. Marcie watched Ellen watching Buzz watching her and came to the conclusion that romantic love was a cruel trick that nature had inflicted on the hapless human race. So far, from what she'd experienced and observed, it wasn't worth the heartbreak.

Out of the corner of her eye, she caught glimpses of Gentleman Jim mingling with his guests. But, after all, it was hard not to notice someone who towered over most of the people in the room.

*Just a big, overbearing egotist,* she told herself firmly. *Trust your first impressions.*

## Chapter Three

"Ellen, it's Marcie." She grabbed a pencil with her free hand and scratched *Call Ellen* off the list taped to the wall beside her phone. "I needed to hear a rational human voice. I've been talking nonstop to the cats, but they aren't much help. Listen, will you be free for lunch Wednesday or Thursday?"

"Bad weekend?" Ellen asked sympathetically. "Sure. Buzz won't miss me for an hour or two, either day. Actually, I doubt if he'd even know I was gone if I left for a week, except that he'd wonder why the advertising bills hadn't been sent out."

The relationship between Buzz and Ellen had been on Marcie's mind a great deal during the past few days. Thinking about their feelings for each other kept her— at least part of the time—from thinking about her own feelings, which seemed a very good idea, given her attraction to the wholly unsuitable Jim Wolverton.

"That's part of what I wanted to talk to you about," she told Ellen. "I have a screwball idea. And I wanted to thank both of you for dinner the other night."

"You always did have screwball ideas, and you're welcome. How *are* the cats? Did you find out where the calico came from?"

"No," Marcie said a little wildly. "That's part of

43

my problem. They're multiplying like—like rabbits, if that makes sense. I asked my neighbor—do you know Sarita Cox, by the way?—if she'd seen any of them before, and she said something about their being wise beyond our imaginings, like all cats. If they're so wise and she's so wise, why don't they adopt *her?* See what I mean about needing to hear a rational human voice? And there are four of them now. Two more hungry mouths showed up on my front porch last night. I'm beginning to wonder where it'll end.''

''*Four?*'' Ellen laughed. ''It's a zoo out there, Marcie, didn't you know that? Yes, we all know Sarita. Listen to her. She's usually right about things, no matter how strange it seems. And you always did love animals. You'd befriend any stray that came along.''

''Lions and tigers and bears—oh, my!'' Marcie muttered. But Jim Wolverton wasn't a stray animal. Or, come to think of it, was he?

''Are you sleeping all right, Marcie? You do sound a little stressed out. Had any luck looking at property?''

''No and no.'' Her sleep had once more been interrupted by strange cries in the night, just when she'd managed to convince herself that it had all been her imagination. ''That's another thing I wanted to talk to you about. Anyway, I'll unload it all on Thursday, if you're available—and if I can manage to say anything but 'meow' by then. Pick you up at the *Gazette* about noon?''

''Sounds good. Hang in there, Marcie.''

Marcie put the phone down and stood and studied her lists. There had to be some sanity in this world; if she could just organize her lists and her time properly, surely everything would eventually fall into place.

A chorus of catly voices from the back porch told

her it was feedingtime. She looked out warily, counting heads. There were still just four. She sighed with relief.

Jim wasn't quite sure why he was doing all this. He was acting like a fifteen-year-old with his first crush, and that wasn't like him at all.

First he'd stood on his front steps, looking out at the warm, peaceful evening, then at his bicycle propped against the oak tree, then at the single rosebud on the scraggly bush that had survived against all odds at the left side of his front walk. He wasn't much of a gardener, a fact with which he was sure the rosebush would have agreed heartily if it could talk.

The restaurant was closed on Monday, which gave him the evening to himself. Usually it was a great time to kick back or catch up on paperwork, but here he was, dreaming up an improbable scheme to try to impress a thorny little schoolteacher from Chicago. He'd just drop by casually, that's what he'd do, and tell her how much he enjoyed dancing with her the other night.

The next thing he knew, he'd cut that single large rosebud. He'd say one thing for that bush; it had put its heart and soul into that one offspring—and— ouch!—into its thorns. He stared at it thoughtfully for a moment; it reminded him of its intended recipient. But her thorns must be retractable. They certainly hadn't been in evidence the other night when they'd been dancing. She'd been as soft and fragrant and light as a rose petal.

After a few minutes' thought, he'd wrapped the treacherous stem in damp paper towels and then in a section from the *Gazette*. At least it wouldn't bite him that way, and he'd have to carry it by hand. Carefully. There was no place to stow it on his bike.

And there he was, almost at the end of Shore Drive on an evening that was heavy with humidity and mosquitoes, though he hardly noticed those small annoyances. The little house at the end of Shore Drive, that's what Chet had said.

And there it was, and there she was. The light was fading, but she was as vivid as a flame. Bright-yellow tank top and white shorts and sandals—kneeling with her back to him, fiddling with a box of something under the tree. Feeding cats?

A mosquito droned like a dive-bomber behind his left ear and struck viciously on a tender, exposed patch of flesh on his neck. He swatted, the bike skidded, and he flailed out to try to regain his balance. That was apparently a serious mistake. He was conscious of his head hitting something extremely hard, and then it didn't seem as if he were conscious of anything at all.

Until he slitted his eyes open and saw her face close above his, shock and alarm in her violet eyes. He thought she was asking him if he was all right, and of course he wasn't. He closed his eyes again with a slight groan and said, "I reckon." He reckoned that wasn't much of an answer, but it was the best he could manage under the circumstances.

"Can you sit up? No, maybe you'd better not. Not for a minute or two, anyway. Just take it easy." Which was superfluous advice, as he showed no signs of doing anything else. Marcie had dealt with countless playground mishaps and had thought she was always pretty cool in an emergency. This was different. This was not a child, and she certainly couldn't carry him into the house, and there were no playground helpers standing by to offer aid.

"You're bleeding," she said. "Look, I'd better get towels and ice—"

He put his hand up to his head and then managed to push himself up on his elbow, staring at her in the most peculiar way. "Died and went to heaven," he muttered and took a deep breath. "What happened?"

"I think your horse threw you, cowboy." She tried to smile at him reassuringly, but she knew the worry in her eyes contradicted the smile. "We should probably go in and get that cleaned off, but don't move if you don't feel like it."

"I can make it." He sat up carefully, looking at the tweaked frame of the bike beside the stone gatepost at the end of her walk. "Didn't plan it this way." His head and his shoulder throbbed with pain, and his movement had made the blood flow faster from the cut on his forehead.

Still, he managed to struggle to his feet. She tried to help, but that big frame— Even so, she had to try. She positioned herself close to his right side. "Lean on me, if you want," she told him and saw the ghost of a smile that tried valiantly to lift the corners of his mouth. He leaned, but lightly.

And why on earth, she wondered, was he still carrying that newspaper dangling in his left hand? Never mind. All her strength and concentration had to be directed to getting him into the house, into the kitchen. She tightened her grip around his waist and thought that, under different circumstances, she might have enjoyed this.

"There," she said, easing him onto a kitchen chair at last with considerable relief. "Now, we'll clean that up and see how bad it is."

"Thank you. And I'm sorry."

"You look pretty sorry. Now sit still."

He winced, but her touch with the wet towels was gentle, and gradually he relaxed. "I should have watched where I was going, I guess. My daddy always told me I was a klutz. I think I was shot down by a mosquito when I wasn't looking."

"You're not a klutz. Accidents happen." She felt in control now, able to do something constructive, and the fact that he was sitting down made it easier. At least this way he wasn't towering over her, making her feel insignificant.

"It doesn't look as if it'll need stitches," she said after a few minutes. "Still, that bleeding doesn't want to stop. Let me get more ice."

The voice from the back door made her start. "Something has happened. I was laying out the cards, and something came to me—a vision, and blood, and I thought I heard a commotion. Are you all right, Marcie? Oh, dear. It's Jim. Damaged, it looks like. Yes, of course, I'm seldom wrong about these things."

The large, barefooted figure of Sarita Cox, this time wearing a long, flowing white garment with gold embroidery, moved through the room like a clipper ship in full sail.

Sarita's light, quick hands brushed over his forehead and shoulders, and she peered into his eyes with surprising expertise. "Bruises and strains, possible mild concussion. You'll hurt tomorrow, young man. Still, it seems to have been ordained. Marcie got rough with you, did she?"

"I hurt today," he told her without hesitation. "And Marcie had nothing to do with it." Well, that wasn't completely true; Marcie's legs had been very distracting. "Can Chennowah Grove's resident herbalist come up with a cure?"

"Thank you for not calling me that 'resident witch,'" Sarita said, grinning at him. "I'm going to bring a poultice and some tea. Not a cure, but it might help. Don't go anywhere. I'll be right back, Marcie. You get some water on to boil." And she disappeared out the back door as quickly and silently as she had arrived, before Marcie could say a word. Marcie obediently filled the teakettle and put it on the Roper to heat.

"Why should you boil water? I'm not going to have a baby, am I?"

Marcie picked up a fresh towel and smiled reassuringly at him. "Not in my kitchen, you're not. You know Sarita, I take it." She came back to his side and held the towel firmly against his forehead. He had recovered enough to be very conscious of her touch now, of her free hand resting gently on his shoulder. "I didn't realize Sarita was a herbalist."

"I buy all my love potions from her. Ouch!" Marcie had pressed just a little too firmly.

"Sorry. You hit that gatepost awfully hard, I'm afraid. Your knee is scraped but not too badly. Here, hold this towel against your head. I'll get another and some soap, and wash that knee."

If he'd been wearing jeans instead of cutoffs, she thought, he would have been better off. Solid, muscular legs—furry, like the rest of him. She felt heat rise to her face. *Marcie,* she reminded herself, *you're rendering first aid, not giving sensual massage.*

"That feels better," he said. "You're good at that."

"I've had practice."

"You mean men are always getting damaged throwing themselves at your feet?"

"Is that what you were doing, for goodness' sake? How flattering! No, I mean I've worked on playgrounds. It's part of my job description, you know, even when they resemble war zones more than playgrounds . . . there." She stood up and backed away from him, assessing the damages judiciously. "You're going to have a black eye, I'm afraid."

"Thanks. Not my first. I'll tell everybody you did it."

"Oh, come on now—"

"How nice to see you two getting along so well—such wonderful vibrations!" Sarita had materialized somehow inside the back screen door, laden with an improbable array of odd items. She stood still, eyes half closed and nose twitching as if the vibrations had an olfactory quality. "My, it almost makes me wish I were young again!" She smiled mistily at Marcie.

"Tea diffuser," Sarita went on, proffering that item to Marcie. "Let it steep in the water for at least five minutes. It's a restorative brew of my own—rosemary, dandelion, sage, among other things. Put some honey in it, Marcie, and maybe you'd both better drink some too. You look a trifle discombobulated. Here"—she divested herself of another part of her burden—"are proper gauze bandages and tape. And this is most important of all."

She plunked an earthenware bowl containing an evil-looking green, gooey mass on the table. "Plantain, comfrey, clematis, and some secret ingredients of my own devising. Freshly picked, of course."

"I won't eat it," Jim stated flatly.

"I should hope not. It's a healing poultice, for ex-

ternal use only. It will stop the bleeding and help keep
the swelling down. I leave him in your capable hands,
Marcie.''

Jim put his elbows on the kitchen table and his hands
over his eyes. He should have stayed home, doing
paperwork, working on the electrical system—anything but biking out here. It had been a bad idea. When
he uncovered his eyes and leaned his chin on his hands,
a little woozily, Sarita was gone and Marcie was pouring boiling water into a rather eccentric-looking teapot
shaped like a cat.

And four very real cats were winding around his
ankles, talking cat talk. ''You running a herd of these
things around here?'' he asked, trying to pull his feet
back under his chair.

Marcie turned, sloshing water. ''Oh. Sorry. Sarita
must have let them in when she left. They're strays,
except for Nero. Don't tell me you don't like cats?''
Poor, misguided man. He was rough with children and
didn't like animals. She scooped up two of the of-
fending creatures and put them on the back porch, then
came back for the other two.

Her hair brushed his arm as she retrieved the second
pair of reluctant felines. It smelled faintly of lemon.
Shampoo, probably. And that tank top had slipped most
fetchingly off one shoulder. He really wished he were
in condition to appreciate all this.

''Cats are very nice, I guess,'' he said politely to
her back as she deposited the cats outside the door.
''It's just that they seem so furry. And they tickle.''
Another thing that he *could* appreciate, if he just felt
a little more like himself, was that those were quite
short white shorts, and her legs were very nicely curved
and smooth and slightly tan—

And then he realized that, actually, he really *was* quite appreciative. Even hospitalized men could fall madly in love with their nurses, after all, if they weren't too sick. And he wasn't too sick, though he definitely felt somewhat damaged.

She turned and looked at him sharply. That fall had somehow affected even his voice; it sounded slightly husky. She'd better get some of Sarita's tea in him. Then she stifled a smile. Wasn't his comment about the furriness of cats a case of the pot calling the kettle black?

When she put the two mugs of steaming, fragrant tea on the table (extra sugar in his—he seemed to need it) she had to push the crumpled newspaper cornucopia out of the way. She'd almost forgotten about it. "Shall I throw this away?" she asked.

He'd forgotten it too, until this moment. "After all I've gone through to bring it to you, darlin'? Not on your life."

"You brought me an old copy of the *Gazette?*" She looked puzzled, and he could understand that.

"Inside—there's a rose in there somewhere. Or there's supposed to be. There used to be."

Carefully, a little surprised, she unrolled the paper. There was indeed a rose in there—an enormous tangerine-and-peach bud nodding broken-necked at the end of a bedraggled stem. "Oh, poor thing," she said. She was touched, and she sounded it. "Poor, injured beautiful thing."

"Shoot, you didn't sound *that* sympathetic when you picked *me* up," he complained.

"You didn't quite break your neck," she reminded him.

"I tried. Guess the rose is terminal. Sorry."

"It's not terminal. I'll snip the stem off right under the bud and put it in Gram's old rose bowl." She was already stretching up on tiptoe, trying to get something from one of the top shelves of the kitchen cupboard.

"Wait—let me help." He started to rise, a little awkwardly, from the chair.

"Sit still. I can get it." She shot him a warning look over her shoulder, and there was an edge to her voice.

He was not averse to sinking back onto the chair. His sudden movement had made the room spin and fogged his vision. But, oddly, in that very moment he understood something that seemed vitally important about Marcella Newberry.

She wasn't telling him to sit still for his own good— though he'd like to think that entered into it some- where. She was doing it for hers. Sensitive about her size, that's what she was. Interesting kind of reaction— or overreaction. He watched her, bemused, while she trimmed the rose stem and put water in the swirled, slightly opalescent round bowl. There wasn't a thing wrong with her size, really. Perfect proportions, rounded here and nipped in there, just as they should be.

With an effort he made himself look back at the rose and the bowl. The rose floated onesidedly in it, a little like a sickly goldfish.

"It'll straighten up as it opens," she told him, as if she knew what he was thinking. He hoped she didn't know *all* of what he was thinking and did his best to look unlecherous. He apparently was successful, be- cause she added, "And I thank you. Why were you bringing me a rose, anyway?"

If nothing else, she was direct. He wasn't sure he could answer that, because he wasn't positive about the reason. He thought about it for a few seconds before answering. There were so many reasons—he didn't know he could be so complicated. Or maybe it was Marcie who was so complicated. Appealingly so. And it had been an impulse to pick that solitary rose, after all, just as coming here had been an impulse.

"I wanted to tell you that I enjoyed dancing with you the other night. And that I don't always beat up on little kids—only if they need it. And I was hoping you'd . . . be my friend." He grinned at her, slightly lopsidedly because of the swelling in his cheek.

An unexpected little jolt of warmth made her heart seem to expand and skip a beat. She had told herself firmly to trust her first impressions. But those impressions were being subtly changed, or her backbone was wilting, or maybe—just maybe—she was being manipulated. She'd rather think she was neither spineless nor easily manipulated; besides, the accident had to have been genuine. No man would put himself through that to gain her sympathy or friendship.

She averted her gaze. Those amber eyes were looking right through her, questioning, probing, reading her reactions as if they'd been written in Day-Glo colors across her face. "I . . . it was very nice of you. Thank you."

"I reckon I owe you more thanks than you owe me," he said. "Picking me up like you did—"

"Well, not quite picking you up." Marcie was laughing now, an enchanting little throaty chuckle that made Jim want to reach out and touch her. "But, after all, I couldn't just leave you there, sprawled half conscious all over my front walk, could I?" She still felt somewhat uneasy, torn between wanting to soothe his wounds and wishing that he would disappear magically so that she could be alone to think.

She grew serious. It would be best if she *did* have some time to think. "Look, if you're feeling up to moving around now, I can run you home in my car."

"My bike—"

"From the way your bike looked, if it were a horse, you'd probably have to shoot it. I don't think it'll fit in my car, but you will. Just barely. And neither you nor your bike are in any condition to go home on your own. I'll put your bike back in the garden shed, and you can pick it up when you feel better."

"I suppose you're right. But be sure you have it out of sight in the shed. There's some suspicion that Kenny MacIntyre and his nasty little friends have taken up stealing bikes this spring."

"Why on earth would they do that?" He was making it up. Kenny seemed to be a splinter in the delicate skin of a developing friendship, and she wasn't sure she wanted to hear about him at all.

"There've been some expensive bikes missing. And I'd think you'd know there are bike-snitching rings in the city. Kenny has contacts, he has the opportunity, and he has the larcenous soul."

"Doesn't Kenny have parents?" she asked, exasperated. Sounded as if Kenny needed a firm hand, counseling, a shove in the right direction.

"They've tried, darlin'. Kenny doesn't respond well."

"Maybe he just needs a firmer hand."

"Right on the seat of his pants," Jim agreed cheerfully and then wished he hadn't said it. She was glowering at him.

"Do you think you can make it to the car?" she asked brusquely through the glower.

He finished his lukewarm tea—it tasted terrible, but not as terrible as he had expected. He stared glumly at the mug for a moment and then reluctantly heaved himself to his feet. "Maybe the next time I see you, I can make a less dramatic entrance," he said, trying to restore some of the easy warmth and understanding that had seemed to be growing between them before he'd mentioned Kenny. "And maybe we could at least go swimming some afternoon soon?"

She would like that. No, she wouldn't like that. What *was* it about this macho Texan, besides the fact that he was a macho Texan? "I've been swimming early in the day, when I can," she told him, forcing her voice to sound normal. "I stop by to see Sam and then give myself a half hour or so—"

"Sam? Who's Sam?" He looked so darned serious! Could it be that he was slightly jealous—of a frog? But then he didn't know Sam was a frog. And Sam was, after all, a very handsome frog.

"A friend of mine." Jim still looked—disapproving? She turned away, hiding a smile. This man seemed to stir up so many conflicting emotions in her. Ellen had said that nobody knew much about his past. And if it happened to be true, as Ellen had also said, that every woman in town was half in love with him, maybe she should buck the trend.

She could almost hear the ghost of Gram, speaking from the shadowy corner of the room, asking suspiciously just what his intentions were. *Distance, Marcie,* she told herself. *Keep your distance.* She turned and started toward the kitchen door.

Jim put out one hand to steady himself on the corner

of the table. Standing here had made him feel light-headed. He tried to remember just why he'd come out here in the first place. Hadn't it had something to do with a turn around the dance floor, a possibility of a summer romance? He frowned, feeling (almost literally) as if his head weren't on quite straight.

The kitchen tilted slightly to the northeast as he got even with the kitchen door and Marcie. He hated feeling this way. It made him remember the long, nightmarish convalescence after the accident. He found himself swaying and putting a hand on her shoulder to steady himself.

"Maybe I should wait just a few more minutes."

"Do you think so, really?" She looked anxious, but there was something else mixed with the anxiety—a wariness, a distrust.

"I'm not faking," he told her quietly and truthfully. "If that's what you thought. After all, if I wanted to spend some—some quality time with you, I wouldn't choose this way, would I?"

There was truth in that, she supposed. She nodded, somewhat reassured, and moved closer to him. He could feel the warmth of her body and caught again the faint scent of lemon, neither of which seemed to do anything to cure his tipsiness. "Can you make it to the living room?" she asked.

He could and did, allowing himself to be settled in a wood-and-leather contraption of a chair that looked as if it came out of a medieval torture chamber but was surprisingly comfortable. She fiddled with something at the back of it, and he was reclining slightly; she brought a matching footstool for his feet.

Shucks, he'd like to be spoiled like this forever! He wasn't aware he'd voiced the thought out loud until he heard her telling him, in no uncertain terms, to put the thought out of his mind.

"The chair is my great-grandfather's Morris chair," she told him, amused at the blissful expression on his face. "I always thought it had magical healing properties when I was a kid. Sit back in it, and all your troubles melt away. And I don't let just *anybody* sit in it, you know—only people who injure themselves flying headfirst into my gatepost." She turned on a lamp on a low table beside him and sat down on the edge of the sofa, leaning forward to watch him closely with her head propped on her left hand.

"In that case, after tonight I promise never to sit in it again. Which is a pity, in one way. It's such a nice room, full of such comfortable old things." And it was. He turned his head a bit, taking it all in. There was no doubt it was an old family house, full of the loving, sentimental acquisitions of generations. Something about it made him feel a little empty and sad. He forced himself to look back at Marcie and smile.

"Are you beginning to feel better?" She hoped he was. She hoped desperately that he was, so that she could take him home soon and get rid of the temptation that he represented: she wanted to put her arms around him and hold that bruised head against her and smooth away the hurt.

*Darn it, Marcie,* she scolded herself, *you always were a sucker for an injured animal. And you know very well that one should never trust an injured animal too far—they're unpredictable.*

"That's a Mikado," he was saying. She herded back her straying thoughts with difficulty. A Mikado? Here?

"Oh." She turned to follow his gaze. Of course. "Granddad's model engine—yes. He built that years ago. He worked for the Northwestern when it still ran a branch line through Chennowah Grove. There were Colburns working on the railroad back when it was the Galena line, when the town was only a whistle-stop.''

''May I look at it?'' He was on his feet now. Out of the magically healing chair, Marcie thought cynically. Though she had to admit he was moving very cautiously. Not faking, he'd said. She had to believe him, looking at those cuts and bruises. A feeling of genuine sympathy almost erased her twinges of uneasiness.

''Of course.'' She walked with him over to the bookshelves that flanked the fieldstone fireplace. He picked up the engine model and cradled it in those big hands of his. So gently. So appreciatively.

''He did a beautiful job. I'm a railroad nut myself. I have a huge HO setup I've been working on ever since I settled in here.'' He turned the engine to one side, admiring the detail.

Marcie smiled up at him. He was a human being, after all. ''Look there,'' she said, brushing his hand with hers as she reached across to point. ''The little engineer—Granddad carved him separately and put him. . . .'' Her voice trailed off, and she took a small step backward. She hadn't realized how close together they were, how much electricity there seemed to be flowing between them.

Jim put the locomotive back on the shelf with exaggerated care and turned toward her. When her hand touched his so lightly, a jolt of yearning had gone through him—a primitive, uncomplicated feeling he hadn't had for so long. And she could do that to him so easily. . . . ''It's remarkable,'' he said finally, keeping himself from drawing her into his arms. Not now.

He wasn't physically or emotionally able to handle these feelings now.

"Very remarkable," Marcie said, taking another step back. For a moment she'd thought he was about to kiss her, and that thought frightened her slightly.

He was almost unaware that he sighed deeply. He felt as if he'd been thrown from his bicycle for a second time this evening, and it was worse than the first. How could he carry on meaningless verbal flirtations with half the women in town when they came to the restaurant, and stumble all over his big feet when he was around this independent little lady?

*Don't call her little, Jim,* he reminded himself. *She doesn't like that.* "I think I'd better get on home now," he said. "If you don't mind." He needed rest—and time to think about his feelings and his motives.

"Of course. You still look a bit shaky—maybe you'd better call your doctor in the morning. At least we got the bleeding stopped." She knew she sounded cool and formal, but at least she gave the impression that she was in control of her feelings. But she wasn't, not at all. Small nerve endings all over her body felt exposed and vulnerable, and she didn't know whether she liked that feeling. Exposed, vulnerable nerve endings could be hurt so easily. . . .

They were in the car, half a block from the house, before she thought to ask him where he lived.

"Behind the restaurant." His voice was sleepy and slow, deep and—she had to admit it—very sexy. "There was an old carriage house on the property when I bought it, and I turned it into a small place of my own. Very comfortable. I'd like to show it to you sometime. Sometime soon."

There was an invitation in that last sentence. Marcie

studied the road ahead with great concentration and muttered something inaudible and, she hoped, noncommittal.

"I'd thought"—still in that peculiarly disturbing tone of voice—"that I'd like to see—to see more of you this summer. Lots more." The comment sank heavily between them, like a large brick into a small pond. He felt a little better now—more like that smooth, controlled Jim Wolverton everyone in Chennowah Grove knew.

Marcie's hands tightened almost convulsively on the steering wheel. A strange kind of anger—both at him and at herself—made the color rise to her cheeks. She was glad it was dark; he couldn't see her turn crimson in the dark, could he?

"I'll be very busy this summer," she managed to say. The Personal Challenge concept seemed to be spiraling out of control. Her excuse sounded lame, but he didn't seem to be particularly put off. Not put off at all, actually.

"Maybe I can he'p, darlin'." Deep in the heart of Texas again. "I'm looking for some additional land too. We could put our heads together, so to speak. And maybe have dinner together sometime soon, or a picnic by the lake, or—"

The slight uneasiness she'd tried to squelch all evening, when she hadn't been playing Florence Nightingale, came flooding back, stronger this time. The man who had every woman in town under seventy in love with him wanted to make another conquest. He was just *too* charmingly persuasive, wasn't he?

"We'll see," she said, striving for a tone of friendly disinterest. Was there such a thing? "Nice of you to offer, but of course before we can blink, school will be starting again, and I'll be going back to the city.'' She pulled through the parking lot at the restaurant and eased along the drive that led to the back, jolting to a stop in front of the converted carriage house in a way that seemed to put a giant period at the end of her statement.

"Well, now, of course you will. I understand that. But you'll surely be back—probably often. And it would be a shame to waste a beautiful summer with all work and no play, now, wouldn't it?'' Odd how sincere and logical he could sound.

And how dangerous. A casual, no-commitment summer conquest—that's what he wanted. Something she certainly didn't need.

Strangely, her hand was engulfed in his. She didn't know how that had happened. To her surprise, he lifted her hand to his lips and—how unexpected from someone like Jim Wolverton—kissed her fingertips, grinning at her mischievously over them. And that beard tickled. It more than tickled. What a crazy thing to do!

And then he was easing himself out of the car, rather carefully, but obviously feeling much better than he had an hour or so before. She'd liked him better when he was a touch more humble. "I'll be in touch,'' he said. That devilish grin hadn't yet quite faded. "To thank you properly for all your tender, loving care.''

She tried to steady her reeling emotions. "It was nothing, and I need no additional thanks,'' she said tightly to the windshield. Darned arrogant male! Her first impressions had been right—don't trust him. Or was that a matter of not trusting herself? Anyway, she'd been right. And darn, being right could be a heavy burden!

"Good night—and take care of yourself,'' she told

him tersely, then swung the car away and back out the drive—and didn't look back.

But when she got two blocks from the restaurant, on a quiet, dark avenue where the streetlights illuminated only pools of leaf-shadowed solitude, she stopped the car and beat furiously on the steering wheel with both clenched fists.

## Chapter Four

**"S**o what's all this about your clouting Jim Wolverton on the head with a two-by-four and then nursing him back to life? That's a really radical way of getting his attention."

Ellen was gazing at Marcie innocently over a patty melt that Marcie suspected was sinfully rich in cholesterol and fat but tasted like ambrosia. The sparklingly mischievous eyes that regarded Marcie from under the fringe of golden bangs seemed to see more than Marcie wanted them to see.

She swallowed the ambrosia that had suddenly turned to mere hamburger and tried to smile back at Ellen.

"Don't tell me. He's claiming brain damage, and he's going to sue. How did you hear about that so fast?"

"You're in a small town now, remember? I ran into Sarita at Carson's drugstore, and she told me all about it."

"And just what does Sarita need at a drugstore, for Pete's sake? She seems to grow all her own medications."

"A birthday card for her brother in Milwaukee," Ellen answered promptly. "Now, about this accident.

Which Sarita doesn't seem to think was really an accident. Preordained, she said. Just what does she mean by that?''

''Who knows?'' Marcie sighed. She had a pretty good idea of how Sarita's mind was working. ''Anyway, it was just an accident. He was just riding by, and he hit the gatepost—the case of the bucking bike, I guess.''

Except that he wasn't just riding by. He'd been bringing her a broken-necked rose, hadn't he? She probably shouldn't mention that. Ellen would blow it all out of proportion, make it into a complete romantic novel.

So, knowing she sounded slightly defensive, she gave Ellen a highly edited version of the whole episode.

She certainly didn't want to mention her personal reactions to him—the feeling that she wasn't sure whether she wanted to get closer to him or run for her life, or at least for her sanity. That strong feeling that he was just a cowboy playboy wouldn't quite leave her.

''And that's all there was to it,'' she concluded. ''Nothing for the whole town of Chennowah Grove to get excited about.''

''Mmm. Maybe he was just trying to get your attention. Kind of a funny way to do it, though.''

''Speaking of getting somebody's attention.'' It was the little break Marcie needed in order to change the subject, and she changed it so quickly that Ellen stared at her suspiciously. Marcie had made a list of the things she wanted to talk over with Ellen, and this was Number One on that list. ''You're in love with Buzz—I mean Brian—Maddox. I can see it all over your face and always could. But you've got a problem.''

"Tell me about it." Ellen rolled her eyes. "Better still, tell me something I *don't* know."

"You're invisible."

"Say again?" Ellen asked, looking down at herself in alarm.

"Invisible. To Brian. He doesn't really see you as you really are—you're just there, always helpful, indispensable, admirable, untouchable. You've always been so darned bright and likable that he probably just thinks he's the luckiest guy in the world to have you working with him—sort of like a high-tech printing press. Don't press any unmarked buttons, or it might disappear in a cloud of glittery dust. I think he's a little afraid of you."

"Oh, come on, Marcie!"

"Well, it's true. You have to do something to get him to stop admiring you from a distance, like a nice cold bronze statue. You have to get his attention focused on the fact that you're warm and human and cuddly."

"Like doing an exotic dance in the middle of the newspaper office?" Ellen asked doubtfully. "I don't think I'd care to crash headfirst into a stone gatepost, the way Jim did. Well, it got your attention, didn't it? But you're probably right. Still, even if Brian saw me at last as a warm, human, cuddly woman, would that make him also suddenly discover that he had a long-buried passion for me? And what could I do, anyway, if not an exotic dance?"

"Put a little Tabasco sauce in the relationship, maybe." Marcie leaned forward across the table, as if she really knew what she was talking about, though she thought wryly that she was a fine one to be giving someone else advice about romance, considering what she thought of as her own failures in that department. "Don't be there when he's looking for you, do the unexpected—"

"Set fire to the newspaper office," Ellen put in with a sage nod.

"Well, no—just to good old Brian. You have to get him to see you in a different light somehow."

That advice was good for another ten minutes' discussion, but though Marcie knew it was a good idea, she couldn't come up with much in the way of concrete examples.

"And, anyway," Ellen said finally, "how come you're taking up the role of matchmaker?"

"Why not? Isn't everybody around here doing the same thing to me?" Her jaw tightened pugnaciously, and she stared accusingly at Ellen. "Sarita and you both seem to be trying to throw me into the arms of a cowboy."

"I can think of worse fates. Jim's awfully nice, and he does need someone, whether he knows it or not, and so do you— Sorry, I'll shut up. Let's both back off, okay? But I'll think about what you said. Honest. Maybe I could come up with a Pulitzer Prize-winning story about the long-term benefits of mutually shared adoration for the paper and dedicate it to Brian Maddox, Editor. Though I suppose to get a Pulitzer, it should be a rousingly gritty exposé of local international criminal connections or something of the sort . . . but nothing much ever happens in Chennowah Grove."

"I guess not. Except. . . ."

"Except what?"

"I've been hearing things at night—that was another thing I wanted to ask you about." Number Two on the list, actually. "Screams? At night? In Chennowah Grove? I mean really blood-curdling screeches?"

Ellen was laughing. "The peacocks, Marcie. The peacocks."

"Peacocks? In Chennowah Grove?" It might be an explanation, but it sounded as unlikely as local international criminal connections.

"The Eddlestons have kept them for years. They are a little raucous, aren't they? But everyone's used to it."

"Okay. Peacocks. Extraordinary—but ordinary, I guess. Must keep the Eddlestons awake at night."

"They're used to it. Besides, Sophie's been gone a lot this past year. She has a sister in Springfield who's been pretty sick. Or maybe she just wants to get away from Wes for a while, and I can't blame her. He hasn't improved with the years. He always was a puffy, liver-lipped hypocrite, but the company's done so well that now he's a very *rich*, puffy, liver-lipped hypocrite. The very stereotype of a thoroughly dislikable man."

Marcie remembered him now. A stereotype, all right, and a wisp of thought somewhere in her conscience asked if she herself were guilty of unfairly stereotyping people—like Texans, for example.

But Ellen's description of Wes Eddleston was disgustingly accurate. A question tugged intriguingly at the back of her mind: Who was driving—gliding, really—down the Eddleston driveway late at night while the peacocks shrieked? Wes Eddleston himself, or one of those international criminal connections—or, more likely, a lady friend? Though surely no "lady" would have any interest in Wes Eddleston.

Ha! It seemed there were intrigues, scandals, and very interesting activities going on in town. There probably always had been; she just hadn't been aware of them as a child. Childhood memories sometimes had a misleading gloss of innocence over them, especially when that childhood had been protected and happy, as hers had been.

And that brought another of the questions on her list to mind.

"Do you know Kenny MacIntyre? Is he as bad as Jim paints him?"

"I don't know how good an artist Jim is, but Kenny's a nasty handful. So are some of the kids he runs with. We really could use that social center, Marcie. It might not solve all the problems, but maybe it could help. The kids need positive things to do." She tinkled the ice in her glass of iced tea and looked pensive. "I hope you can find a good spot for it. Your grandmother had the right idea."

"Gram had lots of humanitarian ideas. Once, when I was small, I remember her saying she'd like to establish a refuge for homeless and wayward cats. Is that humanitarian or catatarian? Anyway, maybe she's done that too. Sometimes I do get the feeling that she's still around."

"Still four of them, Marcie?"

"Still just four. At last count."

"The local vet's name is Dave Hardaway, and he's out on Myrtle and Third. He's excellent," Ellen offered helpfully.

"I'll put that on one of my lists as soon as I get home," Marcie promised.

There was something wrong with the electricity. Nothing new in that, unfortunately, Jim thought. The whole darned place needed rewiring. He'd blown two transformers in the past month.

He righted the small engine and put a line of boxcars back on the track, then stopped and stood very still, staring at the small engine, wishing he could get his mind back on track as easily as he did the line of boxcars.

Thoughts of Marcie Newberry had him all tied up in knots. That Mikado had been beautifully made. And so, darn it, was the granddaughter of the man who had built it. She was like one of those songs that gets caught in the convoluted passages of the mind, playing itself over and over until it seems to threaten sanity itself. He brought his fist down hard on the edge of the train board, causing a small tank car to topple down a miniature embankment.

It wasn't like him to be so fixated.

Maybe it was the warmth and feeling of continuity in that little house of hers. That was part of it, anyway. His own childhood had been eventful, but not exactly rich in warmth and continuity.

In spite of having had to deal with a certain amount of bleeding and bruising, being in Marcie's cottage had been like coming home. He couldn't remember having that feeling before. As long as he could remember, wherever he hung his Stetson was home. Even when he and Sandy had married and he'd built that new little house outside town, there had seemed to be something temporary about it. And it had been temporary, all right, for reasons he couldn't possibly have foreseen. He knew in his heart that even if Sandy had lived, it would have been temporary. Like everything else in his life.

He wasn't going to think that way.

And he was going to have to give Marcie a call—
he still had to pick up his bike. He could take his
pickup over and load it on—and thank her again for
her tender, loving care.

Tender, loving care. It could have been even more
tender, more loving—and it was probably just as well
that it hadn't been, because she wouldn't be here long,
and besides, he didn't want anything long-term, did
he? Temporary, like everything else in his life. Temporary, like life itself. He didn't have to call her right
away about picking up that bike, after all.

Ten minutes later he was on the phone, asking her
when she'd be home so that he could get his bike,
asking her if she'd like to go over to Cliffordsville to
the county fair that weekend, asking himself if he'd
lost all his marbles when his head hit that gatepost.


"And to think I said yes," Marcie told Nero unbelievingly. "I actually said yes." She was still standing by the phone, and Nero was twining around her
ankles while Patches sat on the windowsill, vigorously
tonguing the white bib on her chest.

"As it should be, of course," Nero said in a soft
purring voice, and Marcie took a step backward and
stared unbelievingly at the cat.

But, of course, as she'd thought, cats don't talk.
Not in human language, anyway. Sarita was standing
in her doorway, having come up on the porch in her
bare feet, her fulsome body encased head to toe in a
vivid jungle print that was much louder than she was.

"Sorry. Guess I startled you again, didn't I? I seem
to have a habit of doing that." Sarita didn't sound at
all penitent—smug would have been a better word. "I
should take to wearing cowboy boots and stomping,

shouldn't I? Like someone else we both know. But, of course, I won't. So you said yes, did you? The county fair is always fun.''

"How did you know?''

"Thoughts have wings.''

No, she'd been listening at the door, of course. That would be logical, if rather sneaky.

"You look a little upset,'' Sarita said. "And you shouldn't be. Everything is going exactly as it should.''

"Exactly as it should?'' The feeling of having been transported to the center of never-never land showed in the thin, disbelieving edge in her voice. "I can't find land for the social center, I don't quite trust or understand Jim Wolverton, peacocks scream in the night, and the cats are multiplying like—like rabbits.''

"It's all part of the plan,'' Sarita murmured soothingly, her head tipped on one side and eyes slanted as if she were listening to all those thoughts that were improbably winging their ways around her head. "Part of the plan. Watch the lights, Marcie. Watch the lights.''

"That makes it all perfectly clear, of course.''

The touch of sarcasm was lost on Sarita. "It does. It will. I'll bring you some honey tomorrow. I keep bees, you know. Or they keep me.''

Now why, Marcie wondered after Sarita had left, did she feel peculiarly reassured by all of that, whatever it meant?

Going to the county fair with Jim Wolverton meant talking to everybody in the county.

She found that out early in the day. Apparently a big Texan running a popular restaurant was something of a celebrity in the area; the Texas accent was as thick

as Sarita's honey, and he bestowed it warmly on everyone he spoke to, even her.

Although she noticed with some relief that he never
once referred to her as a "little lady."

Even the octogenarian who'd won the blue ribbon
in the quilt exhibit got a sixteen-year-old glint in her
eye when she spotted Jim. Sitting in a vintage folding
rocker just inside the exhibit tent, she dropped the
scraps of fabric she'd been industriously stitching together when she saw them coming.

"Won it," she said proudly. "Told you I would.
Told you the judges wouldn't be able to resist a Texas
Star done the way I do them."

"I knew you would, Em darlin'," Jim said. "Never
doubted it for a minute. You know Marcie Newberry,
Em?"

"Knew your grandmother," Em said to Marcie.
"Fine woman, good friend. Glad you're here. You
quilt?"

"Uh, no. I'm a schoolteacher. In Chicago."

The old woman nodded approvingly. "Fine career
for a woman, teaching. And you be good to this young
man now. He's a special person."

"She lives at Indian Hills Senior Community in
Chennowah Grove," Jim told her when they went to
admire the breathtaking starburst that had won the first
prize. "And would you look at that quilt! Makes me
prideful to be a Texan, it does."

"She comes to your restaurant frequently?" Somehow Marcie couldn't imagine the eighty-year-old bones
two-stepping around Gentleman Jim's dance floor. But
maybe Em just had a passion for barbecued ribs.

"Not often. Sometimes they get a group together
and come out for a meal. Indian Hills really mush-

roomed, with so many people retiring to this area. Pretty active group.''

''You know them all well, then?'' The man hadn't wasted much time insinuating himself into the life of the town, had he? A matter of good business, undoubtedly.

But his next words made her feel ashamed of that thought. ''Well . . . guess I do, at that. I've been putting on a special Christmas bash for them at my place every year since I've been here. Some of them don't seem to have much family, you know, and anyway, an extra holiday party or two's nice for everyone, isn't it? I know I enjoy it.''

''I see.'' She was seeing, as a matter of fact, a side of Jim Wolverton that she wouldn't have guessed existed. She was warming to him, and she didn't want to warm to him. Not too much.

## Chapter Five

Marcie didn't know how it had happened, but they were walking down the midway hand in hand like a couple of high-school sweethearts, laughing together, absorbing the kaleidoscope of color and sound and aromas that swirled around them.

And she didn't feel a bit of resentment.

Darn it, she really *liked* the man. She'd warmed to him in spite of herself.

By the time Marcie was truly aware of all this, dusk was falling, and it was a little too late to reverse the warming trend. Besides, everyone who paused to talk for a few minutes—and that really did seem to be everyone—seemed to respect and like Jim Wolverton. That respect and liking seemed to be extended to her as well—by association, she guessed—even from total strangers.

Except, maybe, from a few young women who seemed to have a spark of envy in their eyes when they looked from Jim to Marcie.

So, she decided, she might as well leave her hand, which felt suddenly abnormally small, in his oversized paw.

What if he did seem to be towering protectively over her? He couldn't help being so tall, could he? And he hadn't called her "little lady" in quite a long time, had he?

"Getting tired?" Jim asked, jolting her out of her deeply inward thoughts. He was looking down at her with a shadow of concern at her solemn silence. "Want something to eat? The Romanos' booth has the best Italian sausage sandwiches this side of Chicago. And there are tables over there under the trees. Go grab that one at the side, and I'll get the sandwiches. Peppers? Coffee? Iced tea? Lemonade?"

"Yes, peppers," she managed after a wild moment of trying to sort out the questions. "And iced tea, and hurry up. I'm starved." There. She'd asserted herself. It was about time.

What's more, he hustled off quite obediently, and she had her hand back to herself. She studied it, wishing it didn't feel so incomplete and forsaken.

She sat down at the table and put her head in her hands, watching him and trying to sort out her feelings.

It wasn't easy to do both at the same time. He stood there in the short line at the food booth, hands on jeans-clad lean hips, shoulders broad under the plaid summer shirt. He hadn't worn his Stetson and boots, but there was still something that shouted "Texan!" emanating from every inch of that long body.

That attractive long body. No wonder, really, that she'd received some looks of envy—but, darn, she couldn't get involved with this man. She didn't want to get involved with any man, thanks, especially this man, and what was happening to her anyway?

She had business to attend to this summer, and a job to return to, and no time or desire to try to tame a Texan. . . .

He turned and sent a lopsided smile over his shoulder

at her as if he'd sensed her train of thought from a distance, which she certainly hoped wasn't the case. She smiled back and then closed her eyes, willing her strength and independence and faith in first impressions to return. But then she slitted her eyes open and peeked at him once again.

He still looked great. Darn.

When he strode back to the table, he carried a tray that was overflowing with huge crusty sandwiches holding enough meatballs and sauce to feed the Roman army—or the Romano army, anyway. He ate all of his and a good portion of hers before either one of them said much. He tended to purr over his food like one of the cats; she suppressed a smile at the thought.

"You've got sauce on your cheek," she said and reached over with her napkin to wipe it away. He caught her hand and held it, napkin and all, close to his jaw, then turned his head and kissed the side of it.

That was the second time he'd kissed her hand, and the second time he'd made her nerve endings all explode in blissful self-destruction. But he couldn't know, could he, that she'd overreact so unexpectedly to such a simple thing? Just what would a real kiss from this man be like?

She suppressed the thought. Sort of.

"Thank you, darlin'." He was still purring, almost as if he *did* know exactly what she was thinking and was pleased about it.

Marcie retrieved her hand. "Welcome," she said shortly. Her hand was still tingling, the darned traitorous thing.

She clenched both her hands together in her lap and made a determined effort to smile a natural, friendly, unflustered smile. "Great sandwiches," she added, feeling her smile freeze under his intense gaze. *Say something, Marcie. Say anything, just keep it impersonal.* But she couldn't find her voice.

"Knew you'd like them," he said. "The Romanos have their own place up in Beloit—best Italian restaurant in a hundred-mile radius. Now I'll bet you'd like a ride on the Ferris wheel."

Well. There he went again, assuming that he knew best, knew exactly what she'd like, and this time he was wrong. She hated Ferris wheels. She hated heights. She hated dropping through space toward the tops of people's heads, seeing the ground moving up toward her.

"Not chicken, are you?" He looked slightly surprised at the expression on her face.

"Me? Chicken? What on earth are you talking about?"

He shrugged, watching her closely. "Well, it *is* the biggest Ferris wheel on the circuit, and some folks just don't like them."

"I'm not 'some folks.'" She glanced toward the huge wheel and the multicolored lights that had just twinkled on to spangle its circumference. It looked enormous, and she thought uneasily about the generous helping of peppers she'd just consumed. "Let's go. Looks like . . . fun." She had no idea she could lie so easily.

He watched her for a moment, not saying anything, knowing that absurd protective feeling that had just grabbed hold of him shouldn't be mentioned or acknowledged. Not to Marcie. Probably not to himself, either.

She wasn't a very good liar, whatever she might think.

"We could go for a walk along the river instead—

there's a nice little secluded path that winds down toward the bridge.''

"No, thanks." It sounded as if it might be the local version of an old-fashioned lovers' lane, and the Ferris wheel might be marginally preferable. "There should be a great view from''—she swallowed hard, he noticed—"from the top of the wheel. All the lights and everything. . . ."

"All the lights and everything" turned out to be entrancing, once she'd settled down and steeled her nerves and stomach to accept the slight swaying and the smooth advance and retreat of the fairgrounds below as the wheel lifted them high above the colorful crowds and then arced downward.

"Like it? Great view, isn't it?"

"Umm . . . very interesting. No, beautiful. But isn't this thing going a little fast?"

He chuckled. "Within the speed limit. Relax."

"I *am* relaxed," she snarled, jaws tight. And her fingers, clutching the restraining bar in front of them, were white.

Why, bless her heart, she was scared.

Jim let his arm drape across the back of the seat, not quite touching her shoulders. She had the wide-eyed, overwhelmed look of a small child in her eyes, and it was difficult not to let his arm slip to her shoulders, reassuring, feeling the softness of her.

But there was at least one thing he'd learned by now, and that was not to treat Marcie Newberry like a child. And, anyway, he had to admit, he'd rather treat her like a woman.

He let his arm move lightly onto her. There was no explosion, just a curious glance upward at him with a sparkle in her eyes that he'd like to be able to translate a little more clearly. Had he been the cause of that sparkle, or was it just the lights of the wheel, the fair, the stars?

It surprised him that caring about the answer to that seemed so important. Such concentrated caring and tenderness toward a woman weren't familiar to him.

"Maybe I've just been keeping those darned stable doors closed too long," he muttered to himself, unaware that he'd said it out loud.

"Excuse me?"

"Nothing," he said hastily. "Just remembering something."

It was at that moment that the wheel stopped. Suddenly, with a nerve-shattering lurch that left them swaying in place near the top of the arc. All the bright, multicolored lights had blinked out too—and that sparkle had disappeared completely from Marcie's eyes. As a matter of fact, they were squeezed tightly shut.

"What happened?" That wasn't quite an edge of hysteria in her voice, but it was the next thing to it.

"Power failure, I think. Probably something just went out of whack. Don't worry about it." He peered down toward the base of the wheel, where attendants were milling around, getting in each other's way.

"Don't worry about it, he says. And how do we get down? Fly?"

"They'll fix it, darlin'. The rest of the park still has power, so it's just us."

"Very reassuring."

"There's an emergency generator. They'll get it going in a few minutes. We won't be up here long. In the meantime, we've got a great view of the fair and the crowds."

"And they have a great view of us," she said, opening her eyes long enough to peek down at the growing sea of upturned faces below them and then snapping them shut again with a peculiar expression on her face.

His hand tightened on her shoulder and he pulled her closer to him, gently.

"Don't do that," she gasped. "You're rocking us."

He'd hardly felt the movement of the seat himself, but he forced himself to sit very still. He wanted to lean back and laugh, but that wouldn't be very polite, and besides, it would certainly rock the boat, so to speak.

With an effort, he managed to make himself speak gently and seriously. "It'll be all right. We'll be down soon."

Marcie opened one eye and squinted it at him. "You're laughing at me."

Now, that was unfair. He thought he was squelching his amusement very well. He shook his head and started to protest.

"Sit still, darn it," she said through gritted teeth.

He was trying, he really was trying. Poor thing! "Look over there at the clown, the balloon seller," he said, trying to divert her. "Looks mighty like someone's giving him a bad time about something."

It worked. Marcie's eyes opened a smidgen, and she glanced unwillingly downward toward the group. Her eyes flew open all the way as she sorted out the tangle of figures. "Uh-oh," she said.

It was an "uh-oh" fraught with meaning, but Jim had seen it as soon as she had: One of the most active figures was a boy, a gangly, familiar young man who had a nasty tendency to lift fishing rods and probably bicycles and—right now—to snitch a handful of balloons.

And Kenny MacIntyre was quick enough and smart enough, surrounded by friends and cohorts in crime, to duck and run before anyone nearby could react. The clown in his outsized shoes could only stagger forward, nearly falling over his own feet, yelling for help.

Kenny and friends were nearly at the end of the midway within seconds. A couple of people made a grab for them, sensing something was going wrong, but the boys weaseled their way through the crowds, with the bright cluster of balloons tracking their progress, and raced directly toward a couple of elderly women who had just emerged from one of the display tents, absorbed in conversation.

Jim Wolverton swore. Competently, emotionally, savagely. One of the women was his friend Em, leaning on her cane, lost in conversation with her companion.

"If he knocks into her—" he growled. "If he makes her fall, I'll tan his hide for him. I will."

He leaned forward, and Marcie gulped as the chair moved again. She could understand Jim's concern, but from what little she'd seen of his friend Em, Kenny MacIntyre was probably very close to being swatted thoroughly with a cane.

The boys, however, brushed past the two surprised octogenarians, disappearing into the dusk beyond the midway. A single silver balloon escaped, wafting lazily back and forth in the breezes, marking the spot where the boys had vanished.

"If I'd just been down there, those mean little mavericks wouldn't have made it. I'd like to shake that kid until his teeth rattle."

"Well, now," Marcie tried.

"Well, now, nothing. Some kids you have to hit up alongside the head with a whiffletree to get their attention, as my grandfather used to say. Kenny's one of them.''

''Look.'' She'd pulled away from him now, very carefully, not looking down. It was time to try to regain rational thought—for his, for her, for everybody's sake. ''I've worked with youngsters like that. Usually there's some way you can reach them, though it can be difficult.''

''Bleeding hearts don't win these battles,'' he said. But at least he said it in an even, rational tone of voice. ''And don't I wish there were some way I could reach him right now, instead of being stuck up here on a brainless Ferris wheel—''

''With a brainless broad who doesn't know the first thing about roping in mavericks, I suppose. My heart isn't bleeding, for your information. I just don't think much of brute force as a way of handling situations, especially where kids are concerned. And just because you're so much bigger than they doesn't give you the right to be a bully. To be intimidating.''

Icicles. There were at least two or three dripping from each word. ''I'm bigger than *you* are too,'' he reasoned. ''But then, to be fair, I guess 'most everyone is. Do I intimidate you?''

She was saved from answering by a lurch of the seat that reminded her only too clearly of where she was. Clenching her jaw and the restraining bar in front of her and staring straight ahead, she felt tremendous relief that the big wheel was finally descending to ground level.

Relief—and something else: hurt, maybe, disappointment, anger—at Kenny MacIntyre, at Jim Wolverton. And at herself for caring, and, she hated to admit it, for feeling intimidated. Because, actually, she *was,* and she wasn't used to it.

They weren't holding hands as they walked back down the midway toward the entrance. A careful two feet of space separated them—two feet and a fathomless gulf. She said she guessed she'd better get back and feed the cats, and he said he had some paperwork to do, so maybe they should call it a day.

After a largely silent drive back to Chennowah Grove, she told him thank you as politely as she could manage, and he said it had been his pleasure, looking anything but pleasured.

Marcie watched his truck's taillights disappear down the road and then scooped up two of the cats and let herself into the house, sinking down, cat-laden, into the old Morris chair to try to think and to heal and to regain a bit of the peace of what should be her private paradise.

It didn't work. The cats scrabbled away from her lap, prowling and meowing around the chair to remind her that it was mealtime, and the chair itself seemed to have lost its old magic. When she closed her eyes, it felt as if she were stuck once again up on that awful Ferris wheel with that awful man watching that awful Kenny MacIntyre.

And she had to get back to earth. She just had to.

Things didn't seem quite so awful the next morning, though Marcie hadn't slept very well.

But a couple of new properties had come on the market, and she put *View prop.* at the top of her day's list, and she had a carefully planned grocery list, and she was trying not to think those useless thoughts that just went futilely around and around—thoughts of Fer-

ris wheels, or Kenny MacIntyre, or—heaven forbid—
Jim Wolverton.

Perhaps Jim had grown up with a very strict, dog-
matic father and had absorbed some of that kind of
thinking, or perhaps he had too little guidance and was
reacting to *that*. And maybe Kenny had an inbred nasty
streak and was incorrigible—or could he just need
attention?

*Knock it off,* she told herself. In the future she'd
simply say no, thanks to any Ferris-wheel rides. And
to anything else Jim Wolverton had to offer. There was
no way he could fit into her future. Kenny MacIntyre
wasn't her problem, either.

It sounded so simple in theory.

Sarita drifted in around ten, her eyes sharp and probing and a tiny frown pulling her heavy salt-and-pepper
brows together.

"Things are just not going well," she said, settling
her bulk into one of the kitchen chairs and accepting
Marcie's offer of a cup of coffee. Two of the cats
immediately took advantage of the prospect of an ample
lap and curled themselves into comfortable furry circles
with purrs at full throttle.

Today Sarita wore a ballooning bright green-and-
yellow-striped garment with a sheen to it that made
Marcie think of a parachute. "Not well at all, and I
don't understand it," she added, scratching the cats
behind the ears absently and looking puzzled.

"I'm sorry to hear that," Marcie said, pouring the
coffee and looking sympathetically at her new friend.
"Is there anything I can do?"

"Oh, heavens, I wasn't talking about myself. I have
a guardian spirit who keeps an eye on me. So do you,

incidentally. We all do, but most people just tune them out, like you do. No, I was talking about you.''

"Me? But I'm perfectly all right.'' If she had a guardian spirit, she thought wryly, it was a remarkably silent and invisible one.

Sarita shook her head at Marcie's offer of sugar and studied her face searchingly. "Not quite. There's a little too much discord in your life, and for some reason I hadn't foreseen that.''

Marcie didn't know what to say to that, so she just smiled and shook her head slightly.

"Oil on troubled waters,'' Sarita said obscurely. "Would you come for a tarot reading this evening? I have a very special deck, almost a hundred years old, that never fails to enlighten. And I think you need enlightening. If you don't, *I* do.''

"You might be right.'' Marcie almost laughed aloud and then came close to politely declining the offer. But something, a nearly inaudible whisper of encouragement, a strange tingling at the base of her neck, made her put her coffee cup down. "Why not?'' she said. "It sounds like fun.''

Strangely enough, that was true. Sarita had a weird way of making Marcie see things slightly differently.

When her neighbor left soon after, telling Marcie she was going to channel all of her positive currents toward Marcie's ultimate enlightenment, the ordinary, logical, understandable world was a little slow seeping back into her rational consciousness.

She went back to her lists. They helped. Until the phone rang.

"I called to tell you I enjoyed your company yesterday. Most of the time, anyway.''

If that was an apology for being so hardheaded where

Kenny MacIntyre was concerned, it was certainly a left-handed one. "And I enjoyed the fair and the food—" She stopped. She had enjoyed his company too—most of the time—but an iron band of stubbornness kept her from admitting it to him. "Thank you."

Her thank you, she knew, sounded somewhat like a robotic recording, but at least she'd done her duty and tried to be civil. Now all she had to do was to keep her mind on the business that had brought her to Chennowah Grove. She didn't have to see Jim again, did she? Didn't have to get involved in any way, didn't have to deal with impulses and feelings and—and nonsense.

There was a short, uneasy silence. "Well," he said. "You're welcome. And this morning I found your sunglasses on the dashboard of the truck. I'll bring them by this evening, if you like."

So much for not seeing him again.

But maybe she could still manage that. "I'm sorry, but I'll be out this evening," she said carefully, thinking of Sarita. "Could you just leave them on the porch, if you want to drop by with them?"

"You'll be out." He seemed to be turning the fact over in his mind; then his voice grew relentlessly cheerful. "Oh, I wouldn't want to just leave them. Thursday would be better, actually—I have to be back here at work by eight tonight, so I couldn't stay and visit with you, anyway. And I'm taking Thursday off, so we'll have all the time in the world."

She was being roped into something—a typical cowboy trick. All the time in the world—for what? "I could stop by the restaurant," she tried, but the noose tightened.

"No, no need to go out of your way, darlin'. I'll

make up a big picnic basket from our lunch-bar chuck wagon, and we can mosey along the lake, and I can show you a piece of property out west of Mason Street that I think is coming on the market within the month. And we can talk about . . . things.''

The heavy Texas accent had crept back in again, thicker and thicker with every sentence: ''things'' sounded like ''thangs.''

''You don't have to do all that—''

''Oh, but I do. I want to. And that acreage I mentioned just might be exactly what you've been looking for.''

That was the irresistible hook, she told herself. Otherwise she wouldn't consider spending another whole afternoon and evening with the man. Still. . . .

''I really don't think—''

''Won't take no for an answer, darlin'. See you at high noon Thursday. And wear your walkin' shoes.'' He hesitated for a few seconds, then added, ''Have a good time this evening.'' He really didn't sound as if he meant it.

Ha! Was the man jealous? Maybe she should have told him that she'd be seeing Sam this evening. She said good-bye sweetly and with a certain amount of satisfaction. This summer in Chennowah Grove might not quite be paradise, but it had its interesting moments.

Sarita's tarot reading was more than just interesting. It was confusing and really not at all enlightening. At least not to Marcie, though Sarita may have seen the unseeable more clearly than Marcie did. There were no wafting tendrils of incense, no beaded curtains, no purple star-spattered hangings to set the scene at Sarita's. Marcie felt vaguely disappointed in that.

But there were three fat candles flickering at odd times in the dusk of Sarita's kitchen; there were the evocative cards and the curious intensity of Sarita herself.

Marcie found herself half believing in spite of herself, staring at the fascinating arcane cards Sarita had so ceremoniously laid out.

"The past influences the future," Sarita murmured. Marcie couldn't disagree with that. "Interferes with it." Well, now, that might be going too far. "See, here, old loves and outgrown beliefs that must be discarded. . . ."

Marcie peered at the cards, hoping for a sudden flash of light.

"The past belongs in the past."

Marcie nodded and stared at the cards, wondering whether it was Jim's past or her own that was "interfering."

"Both," Sarita said out loud as if Marcie had spoken aloud. "Aha! Here, a young person, very young—a foolish young person—and he's between you and Jim, the cause of the discord."

A little nettled, she asked Sarita what Jim had to do with it. One of the candles flickered wildly, almost going out.

"Everything," Sarita said with a touch of surprise. "I thought you understood that." She frowned, fingers touching the cards lightly, as if she could draw meanings from them through her fingertips. "Stubbornness," Sarita muttered.

"*I'm* not stubborn," Marcie grumbled. "Not me."

"Yes, you are. So is he—so is the foolish young person—here we go. Yes. It takes strength to confront strength, and that will happen. Oh, there are clouds, but here is the sun, you see? Light. Watch for the light, Marcie. It matters.''

Sarita leaned back, looking happier than she had when she began. "Keep an open mind, dear. All will be well. The clouds will clear—when you open your mind. And your heart. That, too, is important."

The reading seemed to be over, and Marcie didn't feel particularly enlightened. She went home feeling just slightly out of sorts—but also, strangely, reassured. It was nice to be told that things will eventually turn out all right, even if she didn't particularly believe that.

And she didn't want to think that Jim would have "everything" to do with her future. That was just too darned inclusive.

It made her feel restless, a feeling that the cats apparently shared. They roamed from windowsill to the top of the refrigerator, to the door and back under the table, tails and whiskers twitching. And then they began talking to one another—and to her—in cat talk, and she didn't have the slightest idea what they were trying to say. Finally, at their command, she let them go out, watching the small bodies turn into moonlight-and-shadow mirages that disappeared quickly.

She went to bed earlier than usual, but sleep eluded her. Where was that "enlightenment"? She could figure out part of what Sarita was trying to say—Jim was stubborn, she herself was stubborn, the young fool, obviously Kenny MacIntyre, was stubborn.

Well, if Sarita was right, it would all work out. And then she could get back to Chicago and settle back in.

It seemed a long way away, in time and in distance.

The cats set up a howling that spelled trouble and jolted her back to reality. She groaned and mumbled uncomplimentary things about cats and put on her robe and slippers.

One of the peacocks screamed. The cats tried to outdo it. Marcie threw open the kitchen door and stood there, hands on hips, calling the cats and glaring at shadows.

Surprisingly, her cats returned to her, though all four of them cast baleful glances back over their sleek shoulders toward the amorphous shadows under the trees and didn't cease their talking until they were all herded into the kitchen.

Marcie went back to the kitchen door and peered out at the night. At the edge of the shadows something moved, and she caught her breath.

A huge, long-haired tawny cat sat there, eyes flashing momentarily amber in the light from the kitchen; then it turned and melted into the darkness. She'd never seen such a big cat.

He looked—well, shaggy, lost, unhappy. She supposed he'd join the cat menagerie before many days had passed. Didn't they all?

Back up in her room, she parted the curtains and looked up toward the Eddleston estate. The peacocks were silent; there were no cars gliding surreptitiously down the drive. Everything normal. . . .

When she awoke the next morning, she felt as if she hadn't slept at all. She had spent all that was left of the night before spinning in a dizzying melange of Ferris wheels, fools, cats, lights and Jim Wolverton. She even looked outside around the shrubs and trees for the humongous feline she'd seen the night before. He wasn't there.

Maybe she'd imagined him too. It had been a bad night.

Waking or sleeping, this summer seemed to get more and more complicated. She recited Sarita's reassurances that all would be well and tried to believe in them.

In the meantime, all she had to do was get past the cloudy part, right? Right.

"Had to fill you in on the results."

"The results of what?" Marcie had nearly forgotten all her wonderful advice to Ellen; Ellen's phone call brought her back from a hopeful listing of all the things she had to do, and a second (and more futile) listing of the things she wanted to avoid doing. Such as thinking about Jim so much.

"The results of shaking some Tabasco sauce around the office. It really rattled some of my more feminist beliefs, but I suppose one has to bend now and then."

"What on earth are you talking about? More to the point, what on earth did you *do?* Sounds almost dangerous."

"I suppose it could have been dangerous around someone other than Brian," Ellen said doubtfully. "With him, what I got was a marginal reaction. I don't think I'll try it again."

"Try what?" Marcie's voice reflected her exasperation and curiosity.

"I wore a bright orange tank top—two sizes too small—to the office yesterday. And I'd shortened a black skirt that was already a bit short and tight. And he stared."

"I'll bet he did. Saw you as a woman. Ha! What did I tell you?"

"Only thing is, for a few minutes I was afraid he was going to send me home to get dressed properly.

Then, finally, he seemed to settle back to enjoy the view. At least, I hope that's what he was doing, though he looked away very quickly whenever I glanced at him.''

"Did he say anything? Anything positive, I mean?''

"Not about my clothes. Or lack of them. Just, slightly regretfully, that he'd always admired my good taste in clothes. But he kept looking—and then he got very thoughtful and asked me if I was feeling all right. He looked worried.''

"Well, at least it's a change. You weren't invisible.''

"No, but I felt a little as if I were wearing a Halloween costume to work. One shouldn't have to resort to that kind of blatant behavior to catch a good man's interest, should one?''

"One shouldn't. Normally. But in Buzz's—I mean Brian's—case, maybe. I mean, I don't think you did anything too awful.''

"Thanks for that, old buddy,'' Ellen said wryly. "Like I said, I won't try it again. But that isn't the only reason I called. A real estate ad was phoned in this morning—private-party type of thing. Sounds as if it could be interesting. Thought I'd give you first crack at it.''

"Thanks, Ellen. Details, please.'' Marcie grabbed a pencil.

"Bordering the lake, small building needing minor renovation. Two full acres, in town.''

"Too good to be true.''

"Maybe. No name, just a number.''

"I'll take that.'' Pinning the phone number to the small bulletin board by her phone a few minutes later, she allowed herself a glimmer of hope. Maybe the clouds *were* parting a little.

That pleasant glimmer was dissipated by an unbelievably loud cacaphony of angry territorial catcalls outside her kitchen window. She caught just a glimpse of the giant orange cat disappearing around her gatepost, retreating from the united forces of Nero and friends.

"Poor thing," she said, wondering to whom he belonged. "Come on, guys, *you* all moved in without all that fuss. Be nice. He may be huge, but four against one makes for lopsided odds."

She didn't know why she was defending him—she didn't need another cat. And how did she know it was a *him?* Might be a big mama.

Four sets of whiskers turned in her direction and twitched slightly. Four sets of eyes burned bright and determined. Four tails remained high and fluffed.

Marcie sighed and went back into the house.

## Chapter Six

Jim rubbed at the scar on his forehead and leaned both elbows on the bar at Gentleman Jim's, staring morosely out at the rather sparse Tuesday-night crowd, not even seeing it.

For two days he'd been arguing with himself.

Why couldn't he just leave Marcie alone? Obviously, that would be best for both of them. It seemed to be what she wanted, anyway. And it made more sense than chasing after her the way he'd been doing.

His earlier vague thoughts of having a long-overdue, uncommitted summer romance had gotten derailed somewhere along the line.

She appealed to him much too deeply for that, even if they didn't see eye to eye on a few things. Independent little maverick. But then, he liked that in her.

Still, she'd be going back to Chicago at the end of the summer. She had her life to live. She'd seemed to have done pretty well without him, up to this point. Could he convince her that she really did need him?

On the other hand, Chicago wasn't *that* far away. And they could work out their differences, couldn't they? He'd always been pretty good at persuading other people to see his point of view.

That might not be simple with Marcie, though. But

with time—yeah. With time, as stubborn as she was, she might even have him thinking the way she did.

Given the fact that both of them were pretty bull-headed, they could spend the rest of their lives locking horns.

He shook his head and whistled softly to himself as he realized he was thinking unaccustomed long-term thoughts.

Thursday. He'd just see how things went on Thursday.

If the weather was any indication, Thursday was going to be a beautiful day. The heat of the last few days had been broken by a thunderstorm sweeping across the plains, pulling cooler air in behind it. Jim even broke into song in the shower that morning, something he rarely did.

It appeared Marcie gave him something to sing about.

Now, if they could just learn how to harmonize. . . .

By the time he'd packed up a huge picnic basket with assorted goodies from the lunch bar at the restaurant, he was feeling almost godlike. Of course things would go well—he'd make them go well. He wouldn't say anything to upset her, and who knew where today's picnic could lead?

He smiled inwardly at some of the mental pictures that question brought to his mind.

He even remembered the sunglasses and presented them to her with a slight bow as soon as she opened her front door just before noon. He knew it was just before noon, because he'd been counting the minutes ever since eleven-fifteen.

"You might need these today." He beamed. "Beautiful day. I ordered it up special, just for us."

"*Did* you now?" She sounded downright skeptical, but at least she was smiling. Smiling up at him between lashes he hadn't remembered were that long from eyes he hadn't remembered were so blue, like bluebells, bright under that smooth cap of short dark hair. For a moment he couldn't speak. Did she have any idea what an effect she had on him?

"Come on inside for a minute. I'm ready— Hey, are you okay?" she asked a little anxiously, and he reined in his stampeding thoughts.

"Never felt better," he said and realized it was the truth.

"Then I'll get the cake."

"Cake? I packed a picnic basket—"

"I thought I'd make an orange chiffon cake," she told him. "My contribution for the day."

So maybe she'd been planning ahead to their time together, just as he had done. "I do love orange chiffon cake," he said fervently, with more feeling than he'd intended in his voice.

Turning away from him, moving with curvaceous grace in her cornflower blue shirt and snug jeans, she shot him a gamine smile. "Thought you might," she said cryptically over her shoulder and disappeared for a moment into the kitchen, reappearing with an old-fashioned cake carrier in her hand.

"There," she said, settling the sunglasses on her nose. "I'm ready if you are."

"And I'm ready for just about anything," he said lightly, then bit his tongue when she looked at him with a shadow of apprehension that he could see even behind those big sunglasses.

She didn't quite trust him.

Maybe she shouldn't, come to think of it. But he had determined to be on his best behavior today. This would be a day for having fun and getting better acquainted, and he wasn't even going to *think* Kenny MacIntyre's name.

He turned to hold the screen door open for her and nearly stumbled. His ankles were entangled by a trio of twining cats bent either on showering him with their overflowing affection or trying to bring him down—he didn't know which.

"The herd," he said tersely, nearly stepping on a paw.

"You don't like cats, do you? I can tell."

"Didn't say I didn't like them. It's just that they do get underfoot." He managed to reach the bottom of the porch steps without mishaps. The trio pussyfooted off to join a fourth cat in a patch of shade under the maple tree. "And what makes you think I don't like them?"

"Because they always, always lavish their attention on people who don't. It's a catly trait."

"Dumb."

"Believe me, they're anything but dumb."

She sounded nettled and defensive. Darn, he'd started off on the wrong foot.

"I meant no disrespect to the cats, ma'am," he said formally and with a smile that he hoped would disarm her. "I'm sure you have the smartest herd of cats in Chennowah Grove. I'm just glad I didn't step on one."

She looked him over head to toe, then looked down at the cats. She apparently found it an uneven match. "Okay. I understand. I'm glad you didn't too—you'd have squushed him. Or her." His smile had apparently worked; she looked as if she wanted to drop the subject, though she was watching the cats thoughtfully. "Still four," she said under her breath, sounding puzzled.

Four sounded like more than enough to him, so he didn't say anything more until they'd stowed the picnic in the truck and were on the winding road that led to Tomahawk Park.

"I know a great spot at the edge of the park, right by the lake," he said. "Off by itself, where nobody will bother us."

She gave him a small, quirky smile. Was there still a hint of uncertainty there? He wasn't used to scaring off the women; it was usually the other way around, the past few years.

"Sounds nice," she said and looked away from him quickly. He was suddenly reminded of an old gun-shy hound he'd had once when he was a boy, and he realized how much he didn't know about Marcie.

And how much she didn't know about him, come to that.

Well, maybe they could remedy some of that this afternoon. He'd just have to take it slow and easy and not scare her off somehow.

He eased his truck skillfully down a rutted side road that skirted the park and led toward the lake, talking of neutral things like the weather and the installation of the new traffic light at the southwest corner of the square, an event that had made headlines in the *Gazette* for two weeks running.

She seemed to relax. And by the time they toted the basket and a big blanket down a narrow, overgrown path through the trees to the edge of the lake, that easy closeness and attraction he'd felt between them a few times before was back.

He'd raided the salad bar for fruits and salads, made up thick ham sandwiches on rye bread, tucked in a variety of sliced cheeses and gourmet crackers—and was suitably grateful for the convenient fact that he ran a restaurant. He'd filled a thermos with iced tea and, at the last moment, added a small bottle of wine to the cooler.

"You rustle up a fine picnic, pardner," she said at last, cutting thick servings of the chiffon cake. "I'm impressed."

"Shucks, ma'am, 'twarn't nothin'." He tried to look suitably humble, with only limited success. "Actually, Joe Bender did most of it. He's my cook. And he's never made orange chiffon cake, that I know of." He polished off his slice and leaned back against a tree, seeming to look out at the lake but actually watching Marcie out of the corner of his eye.

"We're going to have to do this again sometime. Sometime soon," he said. After a moment he added, "Just you and me and the birds and"—he slapped at his arm—"a mosquito or two. I really enjoy your company, Marcie. A perfect day and perfect company."

Marcie wondered whether it was just the warmth of the afternoon sunlight finding its way through the trees or if she was blushing. She was afraid it was the latter. She'd have to watch it—she was getting a little too comfortable with Jim Wolverton.

"Thank you," she answered, not looking at him, and then, "Where does it go?" She was genuinely curious, and she realized as soon as she'd asked the question that he didn't have the vaguest idea of what she was talking about. Her question had surprised even her.

"Where does what go?"

"Your Texas accent."

"Why, darlin', does it fade away sometimes?"

"Like a Texas sunset. Or at least, I suppose Texas sunsets fade away. I've never seen one."

"More's the pity. I'll have to show you one someday." He looked torn between laughter and some hidden sadness, and he sighed. "I left Texas behind when I came up here. I guess I tried to leave the accent behind too, until I found out that a genuine Texan running a genuine Texas barbecue house needed a Stetson and a genuine Texas accent to succeed in northern Illinois."

"But why on earth would you want to get rid of it in the first place?"

"If you like it, I'll keep it," he offered promptly, then thought for a moment. "I worked at toning it down in college, when I was doing part-time radio commentary. Then—" He stopped.

"Then?" she prompted.

One broad shoulder rose and fell in a half shrug, and he looked down at the blade of grass he'd been absently stroking between his fingers. "Leaving the past behind, I guess, when I came up here and settled in Chennowah Grove."

She felt instinctively that she was on treacherous ground. There was something here that was hard for him to talk about. "I'm sorry," she said impulsively, not knowing exactly why.

He reached out and took her hand in his, running the tickly end of the grass blade across the back of it. She shivered a little, and he smiled at her. "I don't talk about it much," he said.

"You don't have to."

"I know. But you have a real strange effect on me. I think I want to, for the first time in years." And he told her—about Sandy, and the accident, and his own guilt. About all the time he'd given to his booming construction company, not seeing that his wife was growing ill and retreating into a world of her own. He recited it all in a monotone that was more poignant than any impassioned dramatic recitation would have been.

Marcie could have cried for him. "I'm sorry," she said again at last when he'd fallen silent.

Still— "Did it really help to come up here and try to leave it all behind?" What she meant was, did it help to run away? But that didn't sound very kind or sympathetic. And she was deeply touched that he had decided to confide in her.

"Yes and no," he said, answering her unspoken thoughts. "Running away and starting all over made it bearable, but I've still never forgiven myself for her death. If I hadn't been so wrapped up in myself— Do you know, after she died, I traveled all over the country, trying to find a place that struck just the right chord, that offered me a chance to be a new person, that seemed like—like home? And I couldn't leave the guilt behind."

She moved closer to him, protesting that it hadn't been his fault, that he had to quit blaming himself. And the next thing she knew, she was in his arms, and she was finding out just what a real kiss from this big bear of a man was like. Not a teasing hand-kiss this time, but a hungry, soul-draining kiss that pulled every inch of energy from her body and left her limp from shock waves of yearning and drained rational thought from her mind.

The tips of his fingers trailed across her shoulders and neck, sending a shiver of electricity clear to her toes and causing a roaring in her ears.

But she realized, abruptly and with a feeling of having been dropped to earth from a cloud's edge, that the roaring wasn't internal at all. Jim had heard it too, and they pulled reluctantly apart, looking toward the lake.

A little too close to the shore, a powerful outboard growled and sliced through the waves, sending wavelets lapping frantically on the narrow beach.

"Who the devil is that?" Jim grumbled, then shouted, "You're running too close to shore!" But the man and woman in the boat obviously couldn't hear over the noise of the engine. "Idiot. Glad it's not one of *my* boats." Then, with dawning comprehension, "Oh."

"Oh?" Marcie asked. She'd managed to pull away from Jim, one of the most difficult feats she'd accomplished in a long time. "What's 'oh' mean?"

"It means 'oh, the idiot is Wes Eddleston.' I should have known. But who's that with him?"

Marcie was shading her eyes and watching the boat, but it was pulling away from them now, the noise and general disruption gradually fading.

Thank goodness for that idiot Wes Eddleston. Otherwise, she really didn't know what she might have done next, getting carried away the way she was by this seemingly irresistible runaway Texan.

"It was nobody I know," she said. "I'm not even sure I'd recognize Eddleston after all these years. I remember him as an overbearing slob with a big nose and a bigger cigar."

"He hasn't changed." Jim looked down at her, the

irritation in his eyes turning to softness, and plucked a strand of grass from her hair. "And that wasn't Sophie with him, either.

"No, it was a blonde—much younger than Sophie would be now. I could see that much. My, my. What would Sophie say?"

"Sophie's in Springfield a lot these days. Her sister hasn't been well."

"Maybe he's just demonstrating one of his motors."

"Sure he is. Would you like to buy some beachfront property in West Texas?"

"Poor Sophie. Married to *that*. And she used to be nice to us when we were kids."

"She's still nice. Too nice, maybe. Overlooks things she shouldn't." He reached out and put his arm around Marcie's shoulders, but she sat unmoving, staring out at the bright, dwindling ripples in the wake of the boat.

A locust whirred insistently nearby; a small animal skittered away from them on the other side of the tree. She could smell the rich summery loam of the woodland, the familiar fresh scent of the lake itself—and the dizzying spell she'd been caught up in a few minutes before had been broken.

A dozen contrary thoughts were warring in her mind. Eddleston's apparent playing around made her think of Michael, which made her remember that she wasn't in the market for romance, which made her remember—with an involuntary shiver—how exciting and wonderful it had felt to be in the arms of this big man beside her.

Too exciting.

And though she truly felt sorry for what he'd been through—well, it might be that he'd been partly to blame for it all. On the other hand, it might be he'd

learned and grown and changed. Maybe he was a ben-
efactor to senior citizens and an upstanding pillar of
the community—and maybe it was true that every
woman in Chennowah Grove was half in love with
him—but she wasn't going to join them in that kind
of madness. *Fight it, Marcie. He's strong and exciting,
and so was Michael.* . . .

"Just where were we when we were interrupted?"
Jim asked, pulling her against him. She couldn't resist
resting her head on his shoulder for a moment before
she pulled away.

"I think we were about to go check that land on
Mason Street you were talking about."

"Funny, that's not the way I remember it."

But she was already packing up the remains of the
picnic, a grave, set look on her face. "It's just that
I—I don't want to get too involved— I'm sorry, Jim.
I shouldn't have said that."

"You're afraid of being hurt," he said with gentle
insight. "I'm not a hurtful person, Marcie."

She paused and looked at him helplessly. "I know
that. At least, I *think* I know that." She turned her
head to one side for a moment, as if she were listening
for voices he couldn't hear. "Still, I can almost hear
Gram telling me to be careful and go slow. And Gram
was a wise woman."

"You have a strong sense of family, haven't you?"
He'd given up and was helping her fold the big blanket,
hating Wes Eddleston with every ounce of his being.
If he hadn't interrupted. . . . "Are your folks in Chicago?"

"No, not anymore. They're in Boston. Dad's with
the city planning commission there. We were always
very close, but the family's pretty scattered now." She

tucked the wine bottle into the corner of the basket and stood up, brushing dirt and grass from her jeans. He squelched the impulse to help her. "Yours are in Texas, I take it."

He hoisted the picnic basket and started back for the truck, adjusting his long strides so that Marcie could keep up. It was a moment before he answered.

"My dad died when I was fourteen. He was . . . kind of a wild one, I guess you'd say. Plenty of old ranching money in the family that he figured he'd better spend. Life was a game to him. Joined the rodeo for a while, took up flying—stunt flying, no less—raced cars, took a monthly trip to Vegas, and died when his parachute tangled during a skydiving venture."

Marcie missed a step, looking up at him. "How awful!"

"Mmm. I went to live with my grandparents until I was old enough to strike out on my own. My mother had left us when I was only two."

"Just—left?"

"Just left." There was an edge of regret in his voice. "Guess she couldn't take my dad's peculiarities any-more, though he always said she was a pretty strange one herself. I always had a hard time forgiving her for—well, abandoning me, was the way it felt."

With a background like that, he'd probably be darned high risk for a long-term haul, Marcie told herself severely. Another brick for her wall of resistance. And besides, he hadn't said anything at all about a long-term haul. Probably inherited some of his father's ir-responsibility—and his mother's.

But that was just one side of her mind. The other was whispering that the poor man had had a pretty unhappy time of it, and wouldn't it be nice if she could breach that wall and help him gain some stability?

"I'm sorry," she said softly, wondering how she could possibly be feeling such a strong surge of protectiveness toward a giant Texan who was certainly able to take care of himself quite nicely, thank you.

He seemed to sense her sympathy, and his free arm reached out and encircled her waist, drawing her toward him. "How sorry?" he asked, and a warning bell went off in Marcie's mind. Surely he was just teasing, but there was an undercurrent in his voice. . . .

She sidestepped neatly, staring up into the branches of the nearest oak tree. "There's the biggest gray squirrel I've ever seen," she lied, putting a safe distance between them.

"Probably a Texas refugee," Jim said. Then, with authority, "Get back over here beside me. Don't go another step."

"I beg your—"

"Don't beg my pardon, darlin'. Just move this way before you step directly into that patch of poison ivy."

"Oh." Marcie looked down at the dangerous, rich profusion of tri-clustered leaves and felt a little stupid. She didn't like feeling stupid. "I would have seen it," she tried, but he was just grinning that engaging grin at her and holding out his hand. Meekly, she put her hand in his and allowed herself to be led back to the truck.

She was fastening her seat belt before she spoke again. Her hand felt warm and strangely as if it didn't belong to her anymore, but to the golden-eyed man watching her with such an unreadable expression.

"Is the land you wanted to show me on Mason Street in town, by any chance, with a small building needing renovation, and two full acres bordering the lake?'' she asked. It seemed a nice, neutral question, and it did seem to defuse the deepening awareness growing between them.

"Fat chance," he snorted, studying the road ahead with absorption. As if he, too, wanted to draw back from that overwhelming attraction. "That sounds too good to be true."

"I thought so too. Ellen got wind of something like that, though, with just a phone number. I haven't been able to reach anyone there."

"Lakefront property is high. But if you find out anything about it, let me know. I'd like to move that boat rental of mine closer to the restaurant—having it down by your place is just a little too far away. Inconvenient. I have to hire someone to be there all the time during the tourist season, and it's hard to check on. I've been looking for a place like the one you described."

She stiffened, righteous indignation taking over. "Let *you* know if it turns out to be perfect? No way. I heard about it first." It sounded a little childish, and she didn't care.

"Hey, I'm not going to try to steal it from you. I meant that it might not be what you're looking for, that's all. And I'm in the market for property too."

"So we could be competing, couldn't we? In fact, it looks as if we are." Her chin was set at that stubborn angle again, and she wouldn't look at him. "Well, may the best man win."

Thinking of several things he could say to that declaration, he let it pass, but he reached over and put his hand over hers briefly. "Relax. I don't bite. I'll show you a piece of land on the lake that I do have my eye on after we look at this Mason Street property—if you'd like.''

"Okay." Marcie made every effort to relax, as instructed. But a little frown was growing between her eyes. It really did complicate things that he was looking for land at the same time she was. It could lead to bad feelings, and it seemed to her that their—friendship, was that the right word?—was complicated enough already.

And weren't they going an awfully long way out on Mason? Where was he taking her? In two more blocks they'd run out of paved street and end up in the middle of Roseview Cemetery.

"Here," he said, turning left onto a long graveled drive. "Kind of back in the woods, but fairly level, and the price isn't bad. Belongs to my bartender's grandfather.''

She already felt let down. It wouldn't do. It was too far away from downtown, nearly inaccessible. She had to hold out for something better.

Jim stopped the truck and looked at her, catching her reaction without her having said a word. "Well, yeah," he said. "I guess it isn't the best place for a community center, is it? I hadn't realized how far out it was when Chet gave me directions.''

"I'll have to try harder to get hold of someone at that phone number Ellen gave me. Which," she added sweetly, "I'm not going to share with you.''

"Did I ask you to?" he asked in exasperation. Was she looking for some excuse for an argument, or was it just his imagination? "Marcie, I'm not going to fight with you over a piece of Illinois sod with grass and weeds and old shack on it. Okay? Now, let's go look at that piece of land I *am* thinking about.''

She felt the reproof in his voice—and something else, perhaps a touch of injured pride—and felt a twinge of guilt trying to squeeze its way through the wall of her defenses.

"Truce," she said, climbing back into the truck and feeling the light pressure of his hand on her back, helping her. Darn, did he have to be such a gentleman? Gentleman Jim. "Didn't mean to sound so prickly." She hadn't intended to apologize, but there it was, sort of, and she wasn't even sure what she was apologizing for.

He slanted her a sideways grin, easing around the crumbling potholes and heading back for town. "It's okay. I actually enjoy a good fight. Especially with a pretty woman."

She couldn't think of an answer for that offhand, so kept quiet.

Turning down a side street two blocks from the restaurant, Jim eased the truck to a stop where the graveled road ended in a grassy meadow leading down toward the water.

"This is it. The price is a little high, and it doesn't go back as far as I'd like, but it could be cleared, and there's plenty of room for a boathouse and even a bait-rental if I plan it right."

"But this is Cattail Beach!" she managed in a thin, unbelieving voice. "This was always open to us as kids. We even had swings in the trees, and there's a wonderful little creek full of tadpoles." Memories of a golden time, of butterflies and laughter and innocence, flowed over her, a warm stream full of the ghosts of past happiness. "You couldn't build on this—it shouldn't even be for sale!" She felt as if her memories were being auctioned off to the highest bidder.

"Well, it is, darlin'. Old Clark Crawford died two years ago, and it's for sale. And believe me, if I don't buy it and develop it, someone else will. It may be a narrow strip, but it's prime land. It'll have to be re-zoned, of course, but there'll be a town meeting next week and we'll see what the council says."

"It's probably full of endangered species," she growled darkly. "There should be an environmental-impact study done. Several of them." She muttered something about the Supreme Court, and he would have laughed, except that she seemed desperately earnest about the whole thing.

"I'll fight it," she said clearly, looking directly at him.

"You'll fight it? The rezoning?"

"Tooth and nail."

"Watch out, world. Here she comes, just like a pint-sized tornado."

"Don't be sarcastic. There's got to be some way of preserving this stretch, and I'm going to find it. You'll have to find somewhere else for your darned development."

"I'll fight back," he warned, anger beginning to grow in him. "You're like a little buzzing hornet under my collar, you know that, Marcie Newberry?"

"Is that what I am? Good. You just wait until you *really* feel me sting, then."

She stalked off toward the truck, her back rigid. Shaking his head, he followed. He'd already felt the sting. And he had a hunch he was going to feel it for a long, long time to come.

"I finally got hold of that number you had for the lake property—and guess what?"

"You bought it."

Marcie humphed with a great deal of feeling. "You're a dreamer, Ellen. At that price and from that man? It turned out to belong to Wes Eddleston. He bought it at a state land auction when the railroad closed down. It even includes the old train station—'the quintessential Victorian railroad edifice, worth a great deal.' That's what he said."

"I can just hear him. He didn't mention the termites, rats, and dry rot that have taken over the old place?"

"Certainly not. I didn't tell him exactly who I was, and he thinks he's dealing with a bubbleheaded female from the city. Oh, but, Ellen, it's such a perfect spot. And the station could be restored and enlarged." Marcie looked around the crowded Town Hall chambers. No tall Texan in sight. "Do you always get this many people at a Town Hall meeting?"

"Nope. This should be a good one. The inexorable proponents of progress pitted against the arch-conservatives of the status quo."

"Sounds like the first line of a *Gazette* article."

"It is. Or it will be. He's over there, Marcie, sitting next to the old couple from the retirement complex."

"Who is?" Marcie tried to sound innocent but knew it hadn't succeeded.

"The guy you've been looking for. Haven't you? And I don't mean Wes Eddleston. *He* just sneaked into the back row with a conniving look on his face. I meant the tall, bearded gentleman over there who keeps looking this way."

"Oh, him. Another of the inexorable proponents of progress. I'm going to flatten his big ideas tonight. At least I hope so."

"Before or after the meeting?"

Marcie looked at Ellen suspiciously. "Just what do you mean by that? Why would I want to conquer his overgrown ego after the meeting?"

"Marcie, Marcie. You do leave yourself wide open at times, don't you? Well, good luck. Shall we go over and join Brian in what passes for the press box?"

"Brian's all yours, and do your darnedest. Press him right into a corner, if you can. As for me, I'll stay here as a lone, staunch defender of the status quo. On one piece of land, at least."

But the evening turned out completely different from what she'd expected, hoped, or planned, and she ended up, battle-sparks lighting her eyes, wondering if she should run for mayor or at least city council, so that things could be run more efficiently in the future.

Though that wouldn't work, would it? Because she'd have to become a full-time resident. . . .

## Chapter Seven

In the first place, it took nearly an hour for the mayor to congratulate himself sufficiently on the wisdom and progressive thinking of the city fathers (especially himself) shown so brilliantly in the installation of the new traffic light.

Marcie bit her tongue and swallowed hard—not an easy thing to do simultaneously—to keep herself from suggesting that the input of a city mother or two might not be amiss. There didn't seem to be any of those around.

And she did find it difficult to keep her mind on the myriad small details—endlessly discussed—that should have been dispatched within a few minutes.

It wasn't just the rather incompetent endlessness of the meeting that bothered her. After all, this was small-town democracy—maybe not at its best, but it worked, if limpingly.

What bothered her, really, was that she kept feeling a pair of eyes staring warm holes in the back of her head. She dared a glance over her shoulder at one point, and the amber cat-eyes twinkled a little but didn't look away. She managed a brief smile and determinedly focused her attention on the mayor, who was—at last!—getting down to the nitty-gritty.

117

"We have two parcels of land up for rezoning, ladies and gentlemen," he droned. "The Crawford parcel, A–47, and the Eddleston property, unnumbered, formerly the Galena station. Let's take the Eddleston property first. What did you have in mind, Wes?"

With narrowed eyes Marcie watched the heavy man rise to his feet. "Progress," he boomed. "There's a syndicate interested in the land and its wonderful little station. A chance for this fair city to become a mecca for tourists and sportsmen, a hotel complex with boating facilities and beach and a train museum."

Marcie couldn't stand it. A development syndicate? Hotel complex? For heaven's sake!

She was on her feet before she realized what she was doing. "There isn't enough land there for all of that," she said, surprised at how strong her voice was. "A large commercial venture there would be too crowded in every way and would infringe on public access to the lake." She thought she'd put that pretty well, but Wes Eddleston looked daggers at her, his face florid and his cheeks puffed.

"Young lady, I'm not sure who you are," he interrupted, "but I'm assured by my contacts that this would be a sound move. Are you against progress?" He sounded as if that might be a hanging offense.

And Marcie didn't miss Jim Wolverton's suppressed smile and averted gaze, either. "I am not," she proclaimed soundly. "But I think that land could be put to better use."

To her pleasure, she heard a murmur of assent from some of the people around her.

"It should probably be discussed pretty thoroughly, Wes," said an older man at the side of the room. "Sounds like it would bring jobs," said another voice, while yet a third added, ''Yeah, but who'd pay for a new sewer system?''

Marcie sat down. At least Wes Eddleston wouldn't railroad everyone into compliance . . . and she wanted that land. Eddleston's attitude and his plans had solidified *that* particular matter in her mind. But she really couldn't afford it, and he wasn't going to be open to bargaining with her after she'd thrown a monkey wrench into his ideas.

And what about parcel A–47? She realized she might have just made a serious tactical mistake. She was determined to fight the development of Cattail Beach, but she'd used all her ammunition on Wes Eddleston. If she used the same arguments against Jim's plans, she'd be considered a troublemaker for sure.

She'd backed herself into a corner. The mayor's voice droned something about further study on the train station and the property around it, then went on to the Crawford land.

Marcie closed her eyes. Now what did she do?

A familiar male voice was saying something about a variance in zoning of old Cattail Beach possibly being a mistake. Marcie opened one eye and listened while Brian said all the things she would have liked to have said.

''But I wasn't planning on anything as extensive as a hotel complex,'' Jim protested. He was staring at Marcie, not at Brian, as if he suspected that Marcie had put Brian up to this opposition. She managed to maintain a straight face and a closed mouth. ''Maybe this isn't a good night to discuss this, after all.'' He looked angry, and Marcie felt a strange little pang that seemed to be a mixture of guilt and satisfaction.

*So there, Jim Wolverton. Sorry, but you can't have*

*everything your own way just because you're so big
and so charming and so—*

She only half heard the mayor suggesting a meeting
of the three-member planning commission the next
week, with Mr. Eddleston and Mr. Wolverton invited
to present their cases, and in the meantime, of course,
he, the mayor, would be glad to listen to any comments
the citizens had to make on the issues, and so forth,
and so forth, and so forth. . . .

Not having any particular trust in political machi-
nations, even in small-town America, Marcie tried to
squelch a twinge of apprehension. They'd get their
way—

"Don't worry," Brian's voice said softly from behind her. "We'll get a good long editorial in this
week's *Gazette*. Might all stir up a little excitement in
Chennowah Grove—we need it."

She turned to smile her thanks at Brian—and at
Ellen, who had slipped into the seat next to Brian,
looking at him with open pride and adoration.

But Marcie's gaze was intercepted by the cold glare
that Jim was aiming directly at her, and the obvious
chill froze her smile in place.

A shame, really, she thought, looking down at the
floor and gathering her wits. Maybe we could have
been friends, but then again, that probably never would
have worked. She could hear the mayor officially end-
ing the meeting with the rather peculiar reminder that
the Fourth of July picnic would be held on Independence Day this year, at Chattauqua Park as usual, and
of course there'd be fireworks. . . .

Marcie stood in her bedroom, leaning her head wearily against the frame of the window.

Why didn't she feel the glow of satisfaction that she should feel, having so nicely thrown a spoke into the wheels of the plans of both Jim and Wes Eddleston? With Brian's help, of course.

A breeze began to ruffle through the high branches of the trees outside her window, and she thought she could smell rain. A low rumble in the distance—perhaps a gathering storm; maybe she could blame her vague feelings of depression on the barometer.

And maybe not.

Jim had walked up behind her in the parking lot, making her jump when the edge in his voice touched her senses like the tip of a whip.

"What is it, Marcie? You don't like change? You're afraid of it?"

She turned and confronted him. "I don't like badly thought out change, not in Chennowah Grove," she told him. "Or anywhere."

He was silent for a moment, staring at her as if he were seeing right through her, probing the depths of her heart and mind. "I guess there's a time for everything," he said. "And maybe this isn't the right time."

Before she could ask him just what that particular statement was supposed to mean, he'd turned on his heel and strode away from her, leaving her with unanswered questions and an odd sense of sadness.

She looked across the grassy knolls toward the Eddleston house. A light upstairs flicked off. Sophie hadn't been at the meeting—probably still with her sister. Marcie felt sorry for Sophie. But maybe Sophie had developed coping mechanisms. Marcie wasn't too sure that she herself was very good at doing that.

The wind gusted, blowing the leaves inside out, and white light flickered on the western horizon. From long habit she counted the seconds until the distant roll of thunder reached the town and rolled through. More, louder, followed quickly.

She turned from the window and went downstairs to let the cats in. During nice weather they liked to sprawl on the porch, four semiwatchful guardians of the night. But tonight they were glad enough to come in, to lay claim to the windowsills, the kitchen chairs. Nero, as was his due, claimed the top of the refrigerator.

Outside the wind was whistling under the eaves and tossing the branches against the night sky, and now there were few seconds to count between the streaks of lightning and the explosive crash of thunder. Rain was pattering hard against the west windows.

"Just be glad you're allowed in," she told the cats.

And she thought of the big ginger cat. Poor thing. Where would he go during a heavy storm?

She grabbed a big pottery bowl from under the sink and filled it with dry cat food, thinking of the small lean-to against the garden fence where the tools had been kept since time immemorial. The shed had its back to the wind, just as a cat would prefer, and maybe he'd seek refuge there. . . .

She dodged through the pelting wind-driven rain and put the bowl in the shed, regaining the house just as an ear-splitting crash of thunder rattled the windows.

There'd been no sign of the big stray, but she was sure he was there someplace.

Scattered showers trailed through in the wake of the storm the next morning; by noon an occasional ray of sunlight filtered through to send rainbows sparkling from each droplet clinging to the leaves and grasses.

"The wind picked the cherries for me," Sarita said from the back door. "I thought I'd bring you some." Her sandals flip-flopped across the kitchen linoleum, and she put the big wooden bowl filled with bright crimson cherries in the middle of the kitchen table, watching Marcie thoughtfully.

"Thank you," Marcie said. "Maybe I'll make a pie." She didn't feel in the least like making a pie— or doing much of anything else, come to that.

"You look peaked, dear. Mustn't fret, you know. A good storm clears the air. Though it may not be over yet."

Marcie glanced out the window. "It looks as if it's clearing. Is more predicted?"

"Not by the weatherman. But I have other sources."

Marcie thought better of questioning that statement. Maybe she didn't want to know. . . .

"I saw Jim in town this morning." Sarita paused, as if waiting for some reaction from Marcie, but Marcie just stared glumly at her lists. She hadn't crossed a darned thing off today's list, and it made her feel guilty.

"He said to say hello to you if I saw you," Sarita murmured.

"How nice."

"You're both very hardheaded. But you mustn't be upset."

"Who's upset?"

"Well, Jim was this morning. He was down at the hardware store to get some paint. It seems there was graffiti scrawled all over the east wall of the restaurant last night. Probably during the town meeting. He was looking for Kenny MacIntyre and his friends."

Not that again. "How could he be so sure it was Kenny?"

"Who else? It was, of course."

"You can see that with your—what do you call it?—second sight?"

"No, no, Marcie. The idiot child signed his initials in one spot. Young people do some very strange things. I was one once, weren't you? Oh, but you are still. Not as foolish as I was, though." She was quiet for a moment and then added musingly, "Maybe he wants to be caught. But, one way or another, it will be taken care of."

"That's what I'm afraid of."

"Oh, not by *Jim*." Sarita smiled and changed the subject abruptly. "What are you going to take to the Fourth of July picnic? It's always potluck, you know. Although of course for the past couple of years Jim has contributed barbecued chicken and ribs. Nice person, Jim is. Very generous."

"I may not go." Rebellion, frustration, and resentment began to bubble to the surface of her mind. She felt as if everything were completely beyond her control.

"But of course you will. You might try a big container of cole slaw—that's fairly simple. Oh, but I can feel you're beginning to get upset with me. I'll leave now. Good-bye, cats. Good-bye, Marcie. See you all later." And she was gone so quickly that it seemed to Marcie as if Sarita had dematerialized somehow.

Marcie plopped down at the table and put her head in her hands. "Grandmother," she groaned to the silent kitchen walls, "what have you done to me? And what am I supposed to do now? Did you know what you were getting me into?"

Of course Gram didn't answer. But Nero jumped

onto her lap and butted his head under her chin, purring. It made her feel a little better, but not much.

The week before the picnic dragged.

She hadn't seen or heard from Jim. It was hard avoiding someone in a town the size of Chennowah Grove, but Jim seemed to be managing it. In her defensiveness, trying to protect her easily bruised heart and equally easily bruised memories of her childhood paradise, she had driven a wedge between them.

And that's exactly what she wanted, wasn't it?

Twice she got leads on property for sale and was twice disappointed. This whole thing was beginning to look impossible, and she wasn't sleeping well, probably she was failing Gram, wasn't she?

She even went so far as to contact Wes Eddleston again about his property, but he was not at all friendly—no surprise there—and was holding the line on his price.

"And if I can't get an okay on permits for construction, it's all your fault," he told her testily. "I don't know who you think you are."

"Likewise, I'm sure," she told him sweetly. Ellen had told her that the town was lining up on her side. So maybe, if she was patient. . . .

But her sleep was fitful, and twice she was awakened by disagreements among her feline friends. She saw nothing of the big orange stray, but the food she'd put out was gone—which didn't mean much; her own four could have devoured it. Still, she wanted to think the wistful long-haired cat had eaten it. The intensity of the disagreements seemed to have diminished a little, and maybe there was a developing friendship?

That idea was shattered on the night of the third of July.

For a minute, struggling up through fuzzy layers of sleep, she thought it was the peacocks.

But, no—she squinted at the clock—it was a two A.M. concert of cats, and they really meant business.

It was two-fifteen before she even began to bring about peace. Her four wanted to ignore her—as cats will do—and go on about their business, which sounded murderous.

She couldn't see the stray anywhere, but he had to be there. Gradually she managed to corral her four, under protest, in the kitchen, where they stalked about with tails high, telling her in no uncertain terms that she'd interfered with their fun.

Marcie sighed and went back up to bed at two-thirty, wondering if she'd ever get back to sleep. Standing at the window, she took deep breaths of the soft night air, trying to lull her mind. . . .

Up on the hill at the Eddleston estate, a light went off. Was Wes Eddleston dealing with contrary cats too? Sophie would be back the next morning, she'd heard, in time for the big picnic. In the meantime, Eddleston apparently wasn't sleeping well.

Marcie focused in more closely. There it was again: a car slipping down the driveway with just parking lights, sliding out onto the winding street at the bottom of the hill before the headlights came up.

His boating companion? Interesting.

Crawling wearily back between her sheets, Marcie frowned with contrary thoughts about the perfidy of men in general and some men in particular—thoughts that were unexpectedly softened when the memory of the warm smile in Jim's eyes suddenly appeared vividly in her mind. The memory of his kiss. A nagging feeling that she might have been unfair to him, that she was too defensive. A tiny door opened at the side of her mind to allow a hint of the realization of love to enter, a tiny beam of light that seemed to dance and to grow brighter in spite of her efforts to slam that door shut.

On the nearly mindless edge of sleep, she tried to run away from that light. But, as so often happens in dreams, her feet seemed unable to move and didn't take her anywhere. Instead, she found her dream self standing knee-deep in sunlit meadow grasses along Cattail Beach, and Jim was there, and she heard him say that it was all right, darlin', they'd find a way to make it work. . . .

"Don't worry, darlin'—we'll find a way to make it work." Jim's voice came from behind her left shoulder in tones that made Marcie's half dreams of the night before flash vividly across her mind. Momentarily she froze, then determinedly grabbed the end of the picnic table.

"Darned things won't line up," she grumbled. She'd been trying to spread an enormous paper table-cloth over three of the park's tables, but the end of one battered table tilted at least three inches beneath the end of the other, and at an angle that would send deviled eggs or pickles or punch into the lap of whoever tried to sit there.

"Patience, darlin'," Jim said, as if he were talking to a small child. She set her jaw and gave the table another tug, deliberately not looking up at him. She didn't want him to see, in her eyes, the tingling uncertain turmoil in her heart.

No. There were too many obstacles—it wouldn't work. *Be strong, Marcie,* she told herself.

"It should be smooth and even," she said between her teeth. "I like things smooth and even and neat." She realized how silly and prim that sounded and mentally kicked herself, sneaking a look at him to see if he was going to laugh at her.

He didn't. His eyes swept over her brightly patterned, wide-necked knit top, her smooth denim shorts, her tanned legs. His gaze settled at last—after what seemed an eternity to Marcie—on one pale-pink polished toenail that peeked from her multicolored sandals.

"I've noticed that about you." He took a deep breath and looked back into her eyes. "Smooth and even, meaning things going your way, if I'm not mistaken. Not very open to negotiation. Downright stubborn, actually."

Darn the man and his superior attitude, reading off a list of her failings like that. And was he right? Of course not. How could she possibly have thought, in the middle of the night, that she might possibly care about him? "You're mistaken," she said, her frustration edging her voice, looking away from those eyes that did such strange things to her senses. "Projecting your own failings on someone else. *I* know how to compromise."

He bent to jam a wedge of wood under the table legs. "There. Neat and smooth and even, right?" He stood and looked down at her, and she risked a sideways glance up at him. The smile in his eyes was enough to melt all the little cold places around her heart. Maybe he'd just been teasing her, trying to make her react. And it had succeeded, hadn't it?

"Thank you," she said in a small voice that didn't sound like her own.

"Maybe we should investigate that word 'compromise,' Marcie. It's a nice word, don't you think?"

She opened her mouth and closed it again with the feeling that no matter what she said, it would mean trouble. The tables might be smooth and even, but all her rationalizations had been jolted out of alignment.

But she was saved from the enormous problem of answering him by a breathless urchin with a dirty face. "Mr. Wolverton? Bill's been looking all over for you. The rotisserie's stuck, and he says to tell you the pig's gettin' sunburned on one side and charred on the other and he needs your help."

Jim muttered a word that Marcie hoped the small boy didn't catch. "Tell him I'll be right there, then," he told the child without looking at him. He still stared at Marcie with a look she wished she could decipher. "We'll talk later, Marcie."

"About what?" she asked, a little suspiciously, before she could stop herself.

"About crooked beat-up picnic tables and park rotisseries that don't work and the need for a few extra tax dollars that *some* new development might bring—not Wes Eddleston's overblown ideas, but well-planned progress that Chennowah Grove could use. And compromises. Among other things." He turned and strode away from her.

She felt deflated, let down, slightly angry, and trying to let the anger overcome the other emotions didn't work very well. The battle wasn't over yet, and she really didn't feel like fighting.

He wanted her to see things his way, of course. Men always did that.

But he couldn't ruin Cattail Beach, the meadow, her memories—she wouldn't let him. Compromise? How? She tried to raise her usually volatile level of righteous indignation to a combative level, but seemed curiously flat.

"Shoot," Marcie said, and gave the beautifully level tablecloth a final, despairing tug.

"I'm going to get very brave and take one of those little canoes out. Aren't they cute? All colors—and they say they're easy to handle."

"But you don't like small boats, Ellen," Marcie reminded her friend. "You always avoided boats and swimming. If I remember right, you said if the Good Lord wanted us to splash around in the water, he'd have given us fins, flippers, and gills. I always figured"—she gave her friend a sly look—"that you just wanted to sit on the beach in a teensy suit and attract the guys."

"I did not. Well, maybe sometimes. It worked, didn't it? And, after all, a lot of the time you were sitting right there beside me, dry as a bone and in a suit even teensier, remember?" The two of them giggled like the fourteen-year-olds they'd once been. "I really never did learn to swim—it just didn't seem important. But the lake is so calm today. And they give you instructions before you go out. And I could stay close to shore. They'll hold two people. Want to go out with me?"

"Maybe. I told Sarita I'd help her out at the salad table. Why don't you take Brian with you?"

Ellen sighed. "He's busy talking to a lot of Very Important People today. I don't seem to be one of them. If wishes were horses. . . ."

"Oh, my dear—I was so afraid for you, but I see such a wonder. Just when all seems lost, you will be lifted into the rainbow on the arms of love, and your wishes will come true." Sarita's husky voice drifted between them like a celestial breeze.

"Wonderful—I always did adore rainbows. How come you're always the bearer of good tidings, Sarita? You hardly ever predict thunderbolts and strife," Ellen said.

Sarita gave her a withering look. "I try to see the best, and besides, nobody wants to hear bad news. So I keep it to myself. Though," she added darkly, "I won't say I never see problems. Problems are part of life, aren't they? But I do like what I see for you."

Ellen chuckled and blew a thank-you kiss at Sarita, who stood before them, majestically resplendent in a red, white, and blue caftan liberally scattered with stars. "Should I believe you?"

"Believe me. Have I lied to you yet?" Sarita's voice had returned to normal, and she looked indignantly at Ellen, then at Marcie. "I've come to free you from Ellen's snares of skepticism, Marcie. One thousand pickles are begging to be decanted."

"I can hear them from here. See you later, Ellen." Marcie followed Sarita obediently back to the salad table, hoping that Sarita was right—about Ellen's future, not about talking pickles.

There had to be more than a thousand, Marcie thought a half hour later: thousands of pickles, olives, home-grown tomatoes to be sliced, gallons of dressing to be poured over salads in tubs. Huge containers of cole slaw—her own among them—and potato salad, macaroni salad, fruit salads crowded the long tables.

She'd never seen so much food in all her life.

She could hear outboard motors on the lake, the clang of the horseshoes from the horseshoe pit. For a moment she was transported back to other Fourth of July celebrations in Chennowah Grove.

Granddad had loved horseshoes. But he was gone, and Gram was gone—and this was now. She squeezed her eyes shut against the changes, but they were real. Twenty years of changes.

Intellectually she could accept that. Emotionally? Maybe.

The luscious aroma of roast pig wafted over from the barbecue area, not seeming at all charred—just nice and crispy around the edges. The official "feed," she'd heard, would start in an hour's time. Though it seemed as if everyone, herself included, had been eating most of the day. At least *some* things hadn't changed.

Marcie caught glimpses of Jim's Stetson from time to time, moving among the crowds. He'd apparently done a good job of fixing the rotisserie mechanism. She found herself wishing she were at his side, talking to people, helping everything move smoothly—

Mr. Fixit. Why did he have to seem so perfect?

She thought she saw Kenny MacIntyre in a small group of boys about his age, pushing through the throngs, part of the festivities and yet not part of them. The group blustered past the salad table, and half a dozen pickles disappeared with them.

"Pity," she said, hardly realizing she'd spoken aloud.

"Yes, it is," Sarita said. "Kenny can throw a base-ball with the best of them. He wastes his gifts." She looked at Marcie thoughtfully. "He'll learn, but I have a feeling that his head and heart are still full of mischief. And he's not the only one.''

Before Marcie, startled at her tone, could ask what she was talking about, she realized that Wes Eddleston had come up quietly and was standing not three feet from her.

''Miss Newberry, I'd like to talk to you.'' There was a forced courtesy in his tone, a conciliatory note. A head and heart full of mischief—no, more than mischief. Duplicity, greed, selfishness. Still, what did he want?

''Yes?'' she asked warily and allowed herself to be led away from the watchful gaze of Sarita to the trees that stood behind the picnic tables.

Sarita was not the only one who watched Marcie and Wes drift toward a spot of comparative solitude in the shadows.

Jim had been on the verge of asking Marcie if she'd eat with him, and stopped beyond the salad tables with eyes full of questions. What could she possibly be doing, walking off with Eddleston like that? He felt a surge of protectiveness. Wes Eddleston, for reasons that totally eluded Jim, seemed to have a streak of easy charm that he could summon up if a pretty woman caught his eye.

Has to be his money, Jim thought cynically.

Was Wes going to try to charm Marcie into supporting his plans for the old station property? But it wouldn't work. Marcie wanted that land for herself.

And she was certainly against changing Chennowah Grove in the way that Wes Eddleston wanted to change it. Or even in the slight ways that he himself wanted to change it, darn her stubborn heart.

No. Marcie was much too smart to be taken in by a phony like Wes Eddleston.

Yet there she stood, tiny and dark haired and vulnerable, face tipped up to listen to what Wes was saying. And she looked interested, even pleasant, even when Wes reached out to put a hand on her shoulder.

Jim felt a slight movement at his right. Sophie Eddleston was standing a few feet away, watching too, her face a mask. A tired, rather gray mask.

He glanced back over at the pair beneath the trees, and the protectiveness faded into something that resembled jealousy. Well, he didn't have to stand there and watch, even if Sophie seemed to want to. Kim, his long-legged, bright-eyed hostess from the restaurant, was sitting alone at the end of a bench, staring out across the lake.

She wouldn't be alone for long—she never was. This time he'd be the one who moved in to enjoy her company.

He didn't see the interested, pleasant, vulnerable little Marcie Newberry flare into very visible sparks of obvious fury and stalk angrily away from the man to whom she'd been talking, her eyes full of fire.

But Sophie did, and her lips curled up slightly at the corners.

## Chapter Eight

Of course Marcie was much too smart to fall for any line that Eddleston might dish out. Jim knew that. It was just that he didn't like to see that easy familiar hand on her shoulder.

He wasn't jealous. Not him. Why should he be?

Stopping in his tracks with a befuddled look on his face, he considered that question.

He knew the answer, and the ramifications of it awed him. He was in love. All this time he'd told himself he'd never make the mistake of thinking himself in love again.

The idea that Marcie could be just a summer romance had sounded reasonable at first. So sure of himself, wasn't he?

And then she'd burrowed her feisty, thorny, hard-headed little self right into the middle of his heart, even though he hadn't wanted to admit it.

A glance back over his shoulder told him that Marcie had apparently left Eddleston standing all on his lonesome under that tree, which certainly served him right. For a moment Jim hesitated, thinking of going back to look for her.

But this wasn't a good time and place to declare undying devotion, was it? Undying devotion? What a crazy, old-fashioned thought! The heat must be getting to him—the heat and Marcie Newberry, who was a pain in his neck, a thorn in his side, and a warm jolt of electricity that had pierced right through his flimsy defenses.

Obviously, he was going to have to do something intelligent about this whole situation, though he wasn't at all sure where to start. Thoughtfully, he stood still, rubbing at the scar on his forehead, oblivious to the voice that was calling his name.

"Jim?" He looked up as the voice finally penetrated the muzzy haze that surrounded him. Of course— Kim—she'd seen him approaching and was waving her arms at him, trying to get his attention.

Kim was a good friend as well as an excellent hostess. He'd go over and sit with her for a while, and maybe later, after he'd had a chance to think about all this, he could go round up Marcie and find someplace where they could have a quiet talk. Although he wasn't at all sure how Marcie would react to something like a declaration of undying devotion. Especially from him. She'd probably think he had sneaky ulterior motives.

This was going to take some serious consideration, he decided as he grinned foolishly over at Kim and started toward her. Definitely, he was going to have to talk to Marcie, though he didn't have the foggiest idea of what he was going to say.

Maybe during the fireworks. Maybe they could make some fireworks of their own.

He was still grinning foolishly when he settled down on the bench beside Kim, which made her comment that he had feathers all over his face, and just what had he been up to, anyway?

The excuses he thought up didn't seem to impress Kim, but she knew him well enough not to ask any more questions. Good old Kim.

Good old Kim wandered back with him to the barbecue area shortly afterward. There was plenty of help at every phase of this picnic; small town differences were pushed aside for the day—almost.

"I hear they've decided to turn down Wes Eddleston's plans for redevelopment along the lake," Kim told him as she shifted stacks of plastic and paper plates from cartons to the tables. "Too ambitious, they said."

"They" were being smart, then. But what about his own plans? "Did the rumor factory say anything about the land I was thinking about?" he asked. *Oh, Marcie, Marcie. We may be locking horns again. . . .*

Kim shrugged. "Sounded favorable, from what I heard. But I don't know for sure. Besides, I probably shouldn't be talking about any of it until it's official." Her uncle was on the town council, so she had an inside track.

If Kim said it sounded favorable, it was going his way. The little jolt of optimism that lifted his mood was tempered just slightly by the question of how Marcie would react.

But not tempered much. He was grinning that silly grin again; he just knew it. Somehow he could make everything work out perfectly; he could feel it in his bones.

"You know there might be some opposition, even yet," Kim warned him with a sly sideways look.

"I can handle the opposition, darlin'," he said cockily and draped one arm across Kim's shoulders and gave her a hug.

All that cocky confidence was shot as full of holes as a Swiss cheese when he looked up, out across the clearing. Hungry people were converging on the rotisserie area like bees to nectar, and over on the slope beyond the crowds, he saw Marcie, standing alone and staring directly at him. At him and at Kim.

He couldn't quite decipher the meaning in that fixed, still stare at this distance. Had she heard about the possibility—make that probability—that he was going to get an okay on limited development at Cattail Beach?

Or was she just a little jealous, seeing him there with Kim on such friendly terms? There was a flare of hope that it was the latter. But somehow, knowing Marcie, he didn't think it was. He allowed himself a small sigh. It looked as if his work might be cut out for him, convincing Marcie of so many things. Maybe he should start right now.

"Have to go talk to someone," he told Kim. "It's important."

"No, you don't," Kim told him in a voice that brooked no opposition. "What's important is that you have to supervise getting that darned swine off the spit. I'll be darned if I'm going to do it, and it's going to take a crew of pig wrestlers."

He started to object, but Marcie had disappeared into the throngs of people, and besides, the roast pig had been his idea in the first place, and it really was his responsibility to take over.

He put on his genial Gentleman-Jim-in-charge look and went to face his responsibilities.

Marcie didn't know whether to be elated or furious, so she settled on a little of each.

She could handle unsavory propositions—business

or otherwise—from a creepy-crawly like Wes Eddleston, but what made him try something like that in the first place? That brought little white-hot fingers of fury that nearly choked her. But she couldn't afford to tell him off the way she'd like to, if there was even the remotest chance that she might be able to get hold of that land.

The only answer to his unexpected actions—unwelcome approaches?—that she could think of was that he knew the council wasn't going his way on his plans for development. And that idea brought the elation. By golly, maybe he and a bunch of greedy financiers weren't going to make a killing at the expense of the charm and ambiance of Chennowah Grove, after all.

And what about Jim's plans? Was she being a little too stubborn? Of course not. Still. . . . She looked out across the crowds and saw him, looming bright-haired and broad-shouldered above a group at the barbecue pit. With, darn his thick and tricky Texas hide, one arm draped familiarly around the shoulders of that long-legged hostess of his. That very pretty long-legged hostess.

A natural charmer, wasn't he? She tried to squelch the resentment that burned somewhere in her midsection and went back to join Sarita and the salads.

"Goodness, I missed you. Having a good time? Where have you been?" Sarita was busy uncovering the tubs of salads and putting out gallons of dressings.

"You mean you don't know where I was and whether I was having a good time? Thought you knew everything." Marcie heard the sarcasm in her voice and felt ashamed of herself. "Sorry. I didn't mean that the way it sounded." She reached out and began helping her friend, trying to will away her edgy mood.

Sarita gave her a sharp look. "Mmm. Storm clouds. No, I don't know *everything*. Just most things." She closed her eyes momentarily and lifted her head as if sensing the air. "Besides, with this many people around, the waves and vibrations and messages get all confused." She opened her eyes and gave Marcie a penetrating look. "Doesn't take a psychic to see you're all strung out, dear. It's pretty obvious."

Marcie growled a little and concentrated on the job at hand. This was supposed to be a fun day and, by gosh, she was going to have fun if it killed her.

She finally found a break to fill her own plate, and located Brian and Ellen in a buzzing group at a big table. Sarita wafted beside her, her caftan billowing like a flag unfurling in the breeze.

Well, she just couldn't help but notice, could she, that at the table beside Ellen and Brian, Jim sat with a plate piled unbelievably high, next to a very lovely Kim, deeply absorbed in conversation? Hmph. His Stetson was dangling from a branch above him; his hair caught fiery, dappled sunbeams. How *alive* he looked, vital, masculine! Her fingers itched to touch that bright head, to see if it was as full of electricity and warmth as it looked. She grasped the edge of her plastic picnic plate so hard that she nearly broke it.

And his attention was completely devoted to the woman beside him. Kim had said something that made him laugh; he threw back his head and roared. *The happy lion,* Marcie thought sourly. And then, still chortling, he bent his head to give Kim a quick kiss on the forehead.

Marcie's plate nearly disintegrated.

But Sarita was gently edging her on, and Ellen had caught sight of them and was beckoning them over to the table. Marcie tilted her chin up, managed to smile, and—very nearly—wished she had never come to Chennowah Grove.

"I'm definitely taking one of them out," Ellen was saying.

"Who?" Marcie asked, startled.

"Not who, silly. What. The canoes. That small orange one at the end of the row. It looks lonely because no one has taken it out of the lake for a ride yet today, and I'm going to do it. Want to go with me?"

"She can't," Brian said. "It's a one-man canoe. One woman. Whatever. Anyway, are you sure you want to? You don't like canoes."

"It's the Fourth of July," Ellen said, as if that explained everything. Which maybe it did.

Sarita sat very still for a moment, eyes closed, then opened them and smiled brilliantly at Ellen. "That's fine," she said.

The conversation, it seemed to Marcie, was a bit surreal at this point. Or maybe she just wasn't paying close enough attention. She did feel distracted, sneaking glances over at the table where Jim and his hostess were still having so much darned fun.

"Well, be careful," she said vaguely. "Both oars in the water, and all that. The punch is very good, isn't it?"

"The punch is very gone, at least at this table," Brian pointed out. The big washtubby container in the center of the table was, indeed, down to a few drops. "I'll go get a refill."

"No, I'll go. I need to move around," Marcie said. Maybe if she walked behind the couple at the other table, she could find out what they were talking about.

Not that it was any of her business.

It took a few minutes to convince Brian that she could handle the big tub, but she finally got away from the table and went to the area where the coolers of soft drinks and vats of punch stood.

Darn, the thing *was* pretty heavy when it was filled. She managed to grasp it precariously around the rim and started back.

Sidling around behind Jim's table wasn't difficult. He didn't even know she was within ten miles, he was so involved. She hoped that at least he'd look up and say hi, or offer to carry the tub for her, or give her a smile—but he didn't.

She didn't know what Jim had said just before she got in earshot, but Kim gave him a playful jab on the arm and was telling him he was sure full of Texas something-or-other just as Marcie passed behind them.

She honestly didn't know how it happened. It just seemed to happen so quickly, and it was so satisfying, and she had to look properly embarrassed and sorry and try to find the right words of apology after the tub full of chilled punch somehow slipped forward in her grasp and at least half of it splashed stickily over the unsuspecting pair at the table. . . .

"Oops!" Marcie said.

No, of course she hadn't done it on purpose. Had she?

Jim was still mulling it over in his mind on his way back to the park after going home to change clothes. He'd dropped Kim off at her place; she said she'd walk back. She was still laughing. Thank goodness Kim had a good sense of humor.

His own felt a little stretched. There'd been a strange look in Marcie's eyes when she made those feeble apologies. Once again he wanted to believe she was at least a tad jealous—but, as Kim kept saying, accidents *did* happen. Sure.

Thank goodness his best Stetson had been hanging on the tree and escaped the deluge.

Long afternoon shadows had crept across the rough grounds under the trees when he got back. The softball game was winding down. That rough field really wasn't very good for football or soccer—the town did need new facilities. Marcie's grandmother had been a generous, forward-thinking woman.

The field at the old high school had gone to housing construction after the school was torn down. Things did change, even in small towns. He guessed that was probably kind of hard on people like Marcie, who'd loved it as it was.

She was going to be darned mad if the town okayed his plans for—what had she called it?—Cattail Beach.

It was the commotion at the edge of the lake that jarred him back to the present.

Something was wrong. People were standing on shore shouting, and two or three boats were being dragged out, and someone was struggling in the water offshore. He broke into a run, spotting Sarita and then Marcie in an agitated group at the shoreline.

"What's happening?" He was already past them, knee deep in the shallow water.

"It's Ellen." Marcie was right behind him, grabbing at his arm. "She can't swim. She went out in a canoe, and it just suddenly tipped."

"I'm going after her."

"You're not." Her hold on his arm tightened. "Brian's almost there—you'd just get in the way."

He stopped. She was right, Brian was there, and a

boat was nearing them—it would be all right. He hoped. There was something just a little too limp about Ellen, wasn't there? Had Brian gotten there in time?

"She'll be all right," Sarita said behind him. "Let Brian do it, Jim. This is his destiny."

"His *what?*" he asked incredulously. He turned to look at her, ready to tell her this was no time for soothsaying—but her gaze held him right where he was and chased any chance of argument from his mind.

"In other words, M-Y-O-B," she told him crisply. "This is Brian's show."

Her instructions registered—this had nothing to do with Sarita's usual vibes and visions: It was just good common sense. "Yes, ma'am," Jim answered meekly.

A siren in the distance hinted that someone had called for help. But Jim was pretty darned sure there wasn't any need for that. Brian had brought Ellen to shore, and while some of the concerned bystanders may have thought that was mouth-to-mouth resuscitation, he'd never seen reciprocal resuscitation.

It did seem, judging from appearances, that Ellen would be perfectly all right.

Jim leaned against a tree, pushed his hat back on his head, and grinned. It was about time. He'd begun to wonder if Maddox was a thickheaded blind fool, but it looked as if he'd finally come to his senses. He guessed the threat of losing someone could do that to you.

And thinking about losing someone—he'd lost track of Marcie and Sarita both, and something about this moment made him want Marcie at his side. Where the heck had she gone? Over in that crowd of people around Brian and Ellen? Or just beyond where someone had managed to drag the half-submerged little canoe back to shore?

Then his eyes narrowed, and he stood up straight.

Half hidden by the growing dusk and a cluster of willow shrubs and saplings stood three boys. One of them was Kenny MacIntyre. And Kenny was staring from Ellen and Brian to the dripping bright canoe and back—with a look of something Jim couldn't quite place.

Guilt? Horror? Fascination with near disaster? Or all three? Kenny's friends were pulling at him, trying to get him to leave the scene—and just as Jim started toward them, all three broke and ran.

Well. He was probably just imagining things. Marcie would surely tell him that he was too quick to blame Kenny for any old odd thing that happened around Chennowah Grove.

Still, he wandered down toward the shore. It wouldn't hurt to look that canoe over pretty carefully, because that really was a pretty odd and dangerous thing that had happened to Ellen. Someone had said it just seemed to be sinking under her, then capsized. . . .

He knelt and examined the boat, fingers tracing the holes in the bottom. When he slowly stood, he was frowning. Maybe he was making connections where he shouldn't; maybe he was jumping to conclusions.

But he had a kind of sixth sense that he couldn't explain about things sometimes.

"Got some holes in it, I see." The voice came from behind him, and he turned slowly to look down at the elderly man in his motorized wheelchair. He hadn't even heard him come up; he'd been so lost in disturbing and unpleasant thought.

"Sure has, Les." Les Scott was the active elder

statesman of the retirement complex, which made him very elderly indeed. Jim didn't add that there was something peculiar about those holes.

"Probably snagged on something—branch, dead tree. Shouldn't go out in those things if you can't swim." Les studied the canoe while he tamped tobacco into a pipe that had to be almost as old as he was. "She was a lucky girl—lots of people around and someone noticing what was happening."

"Very lucky," Jim agreed. He was still scanning the trees and shadows, hoping to catch a glimpse of Kenny and his friends. He was going to have to have a very serious talk with that boy. More than a talk. Marcie wouldn't like it at all if she knew what was going through his mind.

"Woulda been a tragedy. But then, like I always say, all's well that ends well." With that original thought, Les managed to get his pipe going and grinned up at Jim. "Lost our bingo caller during all the fuss. You like to fill in until the fireworks start, maybe? You got the best bingo-calling voice in all of Chennowah Grove."

That really wasn't what he wanted to do right then. He wanted to cut a good serviceable willow switch; he wanted to go looking for Kenny, who could be miles away by now.

And he really wanted to be with Marcie, but he was afraid, all things considered, that she wouldn't reciprocate that feeling.

Jim sighed, then made himself smile at Les. "Lead on," he said.

Marcie still felt just a little quivery inside.

The sudden fear for Ellen's safety had cut clear to

the bone, and then seeing Ellen and Brian together—
so very together—had set off a different kind of quiver.

She didn't know that happiness and depression could
be so all mixed up together, but there it was.

"Cheer up," Sarita said softly. They had spread a
blanket in the clearing by the lake, ready for the fireworks; Sarita had hardly left her side since Ellen had
been pulled from the water. She seemed to sense Marcie's mood.

Well, of course she did. She always did, Marcie
thought glumly. Even that was a little depressing. She
felt as if she were being mother-henned. But right now
she needed it.

"I'm fine," she told Sarita. "Just getting tired."

"Jim's calling the bingo game for the seniors, if you
were wondering."

"I wasn't wondering."

Sarita flicked her an amused glance. "Certainly you
were. He's not mad at you."

"Why should he be mad at me? Just because I poured
a torrent of sticky punch all over him?" She stirred
restlessly and studied the toes that were peeking from
her sandals. They'd gotten rather sticky, too, in all the
mess. "Darn, I hate this guilty feeling."

"If you want me to tell you it was an accident, I'm
not going to do it. We both know better. It was no
accident."

"Was too," Marcie said defensively.

"Not very smart, but not an accident. . . . Oh,
look—they're starting off the pinwheels on Murphy's
Island."

For a small town with limited resources, Marcie had
to admit that Chennowah Grove did itself proud in the
fireworks department. As the thunderously brilliant

bursts and sparkles lit the night sky, her mood lifted. Surely everything would work out all right. She oohed and ahhed and laughed with the rest of the crowd, caught up in the vivid celebration.

But then, inevitably, it was over. All that was left was the rather pleasant hint of smoke and the memories and a feeling of letdown. The crowd thinned, and she and Sarita packed up—they'd driven down together— and the sense of anticlimax tugged Marcie's heart downward still another notch.

The park lights were gradually twinkling out, and the happy voices were fading to a subdued murmur. High overhead, a handful of stars gleamed palely, far away, a faint echo of the manmade glitter that had exploded against the dark sky.

"You go ahead to the car," she told Sarita quietly. "I can manage the rest of this stuff." She sighed deeply. "I'm tired, aren't you? And sorry that it's over, in a way."

"It was," Sarita murmured, "quite a long, eventful day. But it's not over. Not yet. And it will never be over as long as you keep the memories."

There were a few memories of this day Marcie wasn't sure she wanted to tuck away. She had some apologies to make, and she was going to have to talk to Wes Eddleston again, even though she didn't want to. She brooded over all the things she was going to have to do in the days ahead, absently watching Sarita's imposing figure glide silently away from her up the dusty path.

She'd have to make some new lists, get things organized in her mind, try to concentrate her efforts.

"I'd offer a penny for your thoughts, but in these days it doesn't seem like a penny goes very far. And it looks like you're thinking some pretty heavy thoughts.''

She jumped. He'd come up behind her so silently, and though he spoke very quietly, the nearness of his voice enveloped her as if he'd actually touched her. For a moment she couldn't move.

"I'm surprised you're still talking to me," she said at last, trying to make her voice light.

"Why, darlin', of course I am. Though I have to admit that I'd rather drink punch than wear it. Besides, pink isn't my color."

"It certainly isn't." She turned toward him. He *was* very close, but she didn't step back as she might have done a week or two before. She couldn't—partly because she felt as if she were enclosed in a magnetic field, and partly because the picnic bench was too close.

"It was unforgivable—"

"You let me be the judge of that. I could forgive you for just about anything, you know. But that wasn't why I was looking for you. We need to have a talk."

"Now?" Something in his voice made her heart do a wobbly flip. "I mean, Sarita's waiting at the car." She looked at him more closely. "You look pretty serious. There's something wrong."

"I've got suspicions along those lines myself. And I've got other suspicions that something's very right. What we have to do is sort out all the tangles and decide which is which."

"Can it wait until tomorrow?"

"I think that would be smart. Since Sarita's waiting for you and it would take me the rest of the night to say everything that I've got eating at me. Maybe even the rest of my life."

Marcie looked up into the depths of his eyes, while

her heart flipped again, clear up into her throat this time. How was she supposed to interpret his words? Panic almost took over as she searched for words and considered possible meanings.

"Tomorrow," he said and put one finger under her chin to hold it tip-tilted up while he planted a light, lingering kiss on her lips. He was smiling when he drew his head back, a slow, heart-melting smile that she could have drowned in. "Tomorrow, and you keep an open mind, now, hear? Now scoot. Sarita's probably wondering what happened to you."

He turned and strode away from her, into the darkness.

Marcie found herself grinning. She suddenly felt wonderful. And he was wrong, of course. Sarita wasn't wondering what had happened to her; she was probably sitting up there in the car, smiling and nodding to herself as if she'd planned this whole thing.

When Marcie finally plopped the rest of the gear into the trunk and slid into the car, though, Sarita didn't say a word. The smile was there, almost illuminating the dark interior of the car with its warm light. Any nodding was imperceptible, and there were no questions. Maybe questions just weren't necessary where Sarita was concerned. Marcie was grateful; she couldn't have put her feelings into words at that point.

They drove home in companionable silence and unloaded the car with few words.

"Sleep well," Sarita said when they'd finished. "That chamomile tea blend that I gave you should help if you have trouble dozing off, and your dreams should be lovely." She stroked Marcie's forehead lightly with a cool finger, then disappeared through the gap in the hedges between the houses, leaving Marcie feeling as if she'd just been blessed.

The four cats were sprawled haphazardly across the porch, looking content and boneless. A whisker and a tail twitched when she brought the last of the picnic things into the house, and Nero made a strange little cat sound in his throat without even opening his eyes, but they all seemed perfectly happy.

Didn't look as if they'd been carrying on their vendetta against the stray, anyway. Where was he these days? Her sleep hadn't been interrupted lately by catly disagreements. Maybe he'd moved on. Marcie would be sorry if he had, poor old thing. He needed a home, even if she didn't really need another cat.

She put things away and straightened up the kitchen. It was already close to midnight, but the number of thoughts and questions chasing themselves around and around in her mind nearly made her dizzy.

Maybe she should have some of that tea of Sarita's, start out on those new lists, and simmer down a little before she took her shower and went to bed.

But the picture of Jim drenched with punch kept intruding into her mind. And the memory of those last few minutes there in the night-shadowed park.

And the thoughts of Ellen and her close call—and Ellen and Brian together—and—

The pencil lead broke.

Darn it, she'd fallen in love with Jim Wolverton, and she hated to admit it. What did he want to talk to her about? It had sounded both good and bad. . . .

The tea seemed to help. So did the shower.

She pushed the curtains in her bedroom aside and stared at the night. The stars seemed closer and brighter now, and a moon sailed fat and low just above the treetops. There was no light at the Eddlestons' tonight. Sophie had been at the picnic. Marcie had caught just a glimpse of her—poor creature, married to that man.

Slipping between the crisp sheets, she felt the whirling of her mind slow. Just a few snatches of thoughts caught her attention as she drifted toward oblivion: Had Wes's zoning requests been denied? Did she have a chance at getting that land—on *her* terms?

And if Eddleston's plans had been torpedoed, what about Jim's? Was it likely that the city would let him go ahead with his? And should she fight it? She wasn't sure she could.

She could never be a child again on Cattail Beach. She had her memories, though. What Sarita had said about memories drifted through her mind.

*First thing tomorrow,* was her last conscious thought. *First thing tomorrow, I'm going to go see Jim. We're going to talk. About a lot of things.*

## Chapter Nine

Marcie had slept well. There had been no peacocks screaming—or maybe she'd just become used to them, like everyone else in Chennowah Grove. No cat fights.

There had been dreams, and from what she could remember of them, they were wonderful. Stretching and smiling, she opened her eyes.

And then she remembered that this was the day she was determined to have a serious talk with Jim. Apprehension took a little luster off the golden edge of the morning, and hope put it right back again.

The way he'd acted last night—he really did care about her, didn't he? Certainly they could work things out. She wasn't quite sure how, but she was determined that they could.

Maybe she should make a list of the things they needed to talk about, of the exact words she wanted to say to him. Although she knew that composing exact speeches ahead of time rarely worked.

She tried making her list over breakfast but found herself writing *I love you* over and over, and that just wouldn't do as the beginning of a conversation. Or would it?

First thing this morning, she'd promised herself, she

153

would go see him. But maybe she could put it off for a little while. After all, it was still pretty early.

Chicken.

Anyway, first she had to feed the cats, of course. And she should call Ellen too and see how she was doing.

"I'm fine. Better than fine. That was one little trick I would never have thought of to get Brian's attention, but it certainly did work, didn't it? I don't think I'll ever have to do it again, though."

"Oh, Ellen. I was so frightened when I saw you go under!"

"It was awful, Marcie." Ellen's voice shook slightly. "So scary. I was absolutely positive that I was going to drown, and at the same time so sure that someone had to see what was happening—and someone did." Her voice grew cheerful on the last words.

"No aftereffects?"

"A sore throat. From screaming, maybe, or from swallowing a ton of lake water. I'll never go out in a canoe again. For that matter, I'm not sure I'll ever want to drink water again. But Brian brought me home and stayed with me all evening, and we talked—well, among other things, and he did most of the talking. And that made it all worth it."

"I'm so glad, Ellen. You take it easy now, hear? And let me know right away when you set a wedding date. I'll try to get over to see you sometime later today."

Marcie hung up the phone, fighting an unexpected constriction in her own throat. Happy for Ellen, a little sad—and the need to see Jim and talk to him was so strong. Why wouldn't that touch of apprehension go away?

*Do it now, Marcie,* she told herself.

Instead, she looked out at the sparkling golden morning and decided that an invigorating swim would be a marvelous idea. The exercise would sharpen her wits, and she had a feeling she'd need them all.

Sam was sitting on his rock at the edge of the pond when she came back, giving her a cold, reptilian stare. She wanted to stop and talk to him, but he simply said "riibettt" before she could get two words out and sprang away to disappear into the rushes.

The "ribet" had sounded to Marcie exactly like the words "get with it," but of course that was just her runaway imagination. She regarded the spot where Sam had disappeared and reluctantly said, "Okay, Sam." No more stalling. Go see Jim.

The phone was ringing when she came in her back door, but it had stopped, and no one was there by the time she managed to grab it.

Jim? Surely it was Jim, trying to get hold of her. She'd hurry and get over to the restaurant. Of course, it could have been Sarita. Or even someone like Wes Eddleston. Or someone trying to sell her a different telephone service.

But no. She felt sure it was Jim. She wanted it to be Jim.

She hurried to dress, but with more attention to detail than she usually did: a rosy-pink scoop-necked blouse and a vivid floral skirt. She had to clean the last traces of the punch from her sandals before she could put them on, and a small twinge of guilt made her pause.

*Had* she spilled that punch on purpose? Of course not.

The sun was high in the sky by the time she pulled her car to a stop beside the wide verandah of Gentleman

Jim's. The restaurant wasn't open yet, and a man she recognized as the bartender, Chet, was sweeping the steps. He looked up to grin at her when she got out of the car.

"Hi, there," he called as if he were expecting her. "He's been trying to reach you. He's upstairs, playing."

She blinked. "Playing?"

"His train layout. Just go through the blue door at the left of the bar and up the stairs. He'll be awful glad to see you, I can tell. Whenever he's all wrought up about something, he goes up to play with the trains. He's wrought."

Marcie didn't know what to say to this, so she contented herself with a simple thank you, then walked in the half-open front door of the restaurant and dutifully went through the blue door at the left of the bar. The stairs were steep, and a humming buzz grew louder as she got nearer the top of them.

It reminded her of the sound of Granddad's old model train. He'd get it out and set it up for her when she was little—she'd almost forgotten it. Was it still in the attic?

But this train layout, she saw when she reached the top of the stairs, was a great deal more intricate and complicated than Granddad's electric train had been. And the man who bent over it, his back to her, the low lights over the table glancing off his bright head, was certainly not at all like her grandfather.

"It's beautiful," she said involuntarily, stopping just inside the cavernous attic room. "Granddad would have loved to come and play with you."

Jim straightened slowly and turned toward her, a

slow smile lighting his eyes. "And you?" he asked. "Did you come to play?"

She felt a traitorous glow spreading over her cheek-bones. "You said we had to talk."

"Mmmhmm." He turned and adjusted a lever on one of the many small boxes that lined the edge of the big table, and the train humming along the tracks behind him slowed, chugging its way sedately through a miniature tunnel and past a tiny village. "I think I'd rather play."

"I'm sorry if I interrupted—"

"Darlin', I think you misunderstood me. You can interrupt me anytime. I've been trying to get hold of you. Come here."

Of their own volition, her feet found their way across the worn wooden floor until she stood directly in front of him—looking up, so far up. Until his arms closed around her and he kissed her with a kiss that seemed to last forever, making her legs feel useless, boneless.

When he loosened his hold slightly at last, she staggered against him, leaning on that massive chest for support.

"Have to talk," he said. He kissed the top of her head. "That's what I said, wasn't it? Have to talk. Now, why did I say that, darlin'? Now that I've got hold of you finally, I can't seem to remember."

"I think," she managed to say, "that's what I came to find out. What it was that you wanted to talk about, I mean." She wasn't sure either one of them was making any sense, but it didn't really matter, did it?

"Well," he said, "let me see. Here, you stand right there, just about a foot away—no farther now—and maybe I can think a little straighter." He smiled at her, eyes alight, and then took a deep breath, and the smile faded slightly.

"Oh, darn, I remember." He shook his head ruefully. "You sure you want to hear this now?"

"I think maybe I'd better, all things considered." But he'd already, she thought to herself, said the most important thing of all without ever saying a word.

"You may be right. And then maybe we can get back to what we were doing." He hesitated a moment, then added soberly, "That is, if you'll want to, after I speak my piece."

"Speak. Quickly." *So that we can get back to what we were doing,* she thought, but she didn't dare say it out loud.

"Yes, ma'am." His hands were still on her shoulders, and she willed herself to listen to his words and not concentrate on the lovely pressure of his strong fingers. He closed his eyes for a moment, as if he, too, were determinedly summoning all his powers of concentration.

"I've got three things on my mind. You may not like the first two, but I sure do hope you'll like the third. First, there's the land."

"Cattail Beach?"

"If that's what you call it. They're going to let me build on it. I'm sorry, Marcie." He reconsidered those words and then said, "No, I'm not sorry, Marcie. But I don't want to do something you'd really hate. I'm going to try to make it a clean, well-thought-out conversion."

"Don't worry about it." She couldn't believe she was actually saying those words. But still—yes, things did change. She'd been changing, hadn't she, ever since she arrived in Chennowah Grove this summer and met Jim Wolverton? "I mean, I'm not going to throw up roadblocks and organize a taxpayers' revolt or anything." She looked down at her toes and back up at him, a fleeting shadow of sadness passing over her memories. "It was such a special place, though," she added.

"I know. At least, I *think* I know how you must feel. And I'll be gentle to the land."

"I know you would be. It's okay, Jim."

"Sure?"

"Sure."

He looked relieved, and she wanted to step forward and wind her arms around him again, but he was still holding her away with those firm hands on her shoulders.

"The second thing is—well, I'm not sure. A little scary. Not something you're going to want to hear at all, judging from some of your past reactions."

"What past reactions?"

"About Kenny MacIntyre. Marcie, I have a strong suspicion that he and some of his friends thought it would be funny to sabotage canoes. I found carefully hidden holes cut—not snagged, *cut*—in the bottom of the orange canoe Ellen was paddling."

"Oh, they couldn't!"

"Oh, they could. Not meaning serious harm, not ever thinking that someone who couldn't swim would get hurt. One of the other canoes had holes cut just as carefully, right in the same spots, but it hadn't been taken out."

"But why do you think it was Kenny and his friends?" She was still fighting the idea, though she knew Jim wouldn't make empty and unfounded accusations. She might have thought that once, but no longer.

"I saw his face. Right after Brian pulled Ellen out. I saw them take off like a gang of guilty outlaws. And I think—now, I'm not sure, Marcie—I think I saw him early in the morning, with his friends, down along the shore where the canoes were beached. I hadn't thought anything about it at the time."

"But you can't prove it."

"Not unless I could make him confess. Don't look so worried—I won't try to torture a confession out of him. But I'm sorry, Marcie, I've got a gut feeling about this. Some kids are just awfully slow to learn. Maybe I'm so sure of it because I was a pretty hard little cuss to handle, myself."

Marcie was silent for a few minutes. "Okay," she said at last. "All we can do is try to find out the truth. Now, what about that third thing you mentioned?"

He smiled. "You're certainly taking all this well. I thought I was going to have to deal with a miniature tornado, and all you say is 'okay'? How did I get so lucky? Did I do something right for a change?"

"The third thing," she reminded him firmly. "You said there was a third thing."

"I did, didn't I? It may be the hardest of all of them to talk about. The third thing is that I have this crazy feeling that I want to be domesticated."

"*Domesticated?*"

"Well, something of that sort. You were right. When I came up here, I was running away from the past. And then I managed to get by pretty well by living one day at a time, just as they came along. I could always pull up stakes and leave, if I had to. No commitment."

"But didn't you have a commitment to the business? I mean, you've been so successful at it."

"Sure I did. But in the back of my head, I wasn't 'home.' The restaurant could be sold and I could move on, if I really wanted to. I never felt really at home anyplace, I guess, until I sat in your granddad's Morris chair. Maybe it really does have magic in it, do you suppose?"

"I know it does. I just never expected it to work *that* kind of magic."

"I don't want to go on living just for the moment anymore, Marcie. I want to plan for the future. I want to make memories and love my way through a few thousand tomorrows."

She didn't trust herself to speak. There was this crazy urge to use the hackneyed old phrase about this all being so sudden. And it was true, it was pretty sudden. And how could she possibly take him seriously?

And how could she not?

She was quiet for so long that he finally said "Marcie?" in a tentative way, as if he were afraid she was about to turn him down.

"I honestly thought you were just looking for a summertime playmate. But you weren't, were you?" Her voice was low, a little uncertain even now.

"Yup," he said promptly. "I was, but I changed my mind."

"What on earth will I do about my job?"

"Quit."

"And my apartment?"

"Move."

"It'll all take so much planning—I don't know where to start. What will I—"

"Little lady, you talk too much," Jim told her and

swung her around for another of those wonderful, long electric kisses that seemed to lift her off the ground— or more than *seemed* to, for she was literally swept off her feet. She didn't even mind that he'd called her "little lady." In fact, she hardly noticed.

And then her left hip made contact somehow with the train board, and the feeling of electricity became very concentrated, painful enough to make her yelp. Or try to.

She had the fleeting thought that Jim's kisses certainly had some odd effects on her before she realized that several things were happening at once that had nothing to do—well, not directly, anyway—with the purely personal electricity they themselves were generating.

For one thing, after a short sizzly sound, there was an ominous silence from the transformers and the no-longer moving trains. And an even more ominous darkness enveloping them, she realized as she reluctantly opened her eyes.

Jim had set her on her feet and moved a few inches back, grumbling fervently into the darkness—words and phrases she couldn't quite make out and wasn't sure she wanted to.

Marcie rubbed at her hip, which now seemed slightly numb rather than painful. "I think we blew it?" she offered helpfully to the darkness and heard a chuckle.

"If you want to put it like that. You're a superconductor of some kind, I guess. Must have touched the transformer."

"Don't blame it on me. I've never blown a transformer in my life. That I know of."

"Now, I'm kind of surprised at that. You generate enough power to light up the whole town of Chennowah

Grove, all by yourself.'' She could hear the smile in his voice, and the gentle touch of his hand on her shoulder was reassuring.

''All the wiring in this place needs to be reworked,'' he said with a sigh. ''And I keep putting it off, so I'm not blaming you. Though I'd say''—his hands were on her shoulders again, pulling her toward him—''that I do get a charge out of you. If you'll forgive the awful pun.''

She was about to tell him that his words were really beyond reasonable forgiveness when the door to the big attic room banged open and a flashlight beam did a fair job of blinding her.

''Hey, Jim! Something sure did it this time. All the circuits are off down there— Oh, sorry, did I interrupt something?''

Jim snatched his hands away from Marcie and turned toward the source of the light. ''Chet, aim that darned thing down a little, will you? I'll get everything fixed, if I'm not permanently blinded. And, yes, you interrupted something. Didn't anyone ever teach you to knock?''

''Knock? But this was an emergency. And besides, the only thing you ever come up here to do is fool around—well. . . .'' Chet's voice was silent for a moment. ''What I meant was to play. To have a little fun. With your trains. Shoot, you know what I mean.''

''It's all right, Chet. We know what you mean.'' Marcie's voice sounded remarkably calm, Jim thought, though he could hear the note of amusement in it. ''Now, if you'd just wield that flashlight in such a way that we could find our way out of here and down the stairs, I'm sure Jim can find all the right buttons to push and levers to pull. He's very good at that.''

"Are you being sarcastic, darlin'?" Jim growled in her ear, following her down the steep stairs.

"Not at all. Just stating facts. Rather nice facts, actually."

"Glad you feel that way. Sure hope that surge of electricity didn't burn out the transformers."

"It nearly burned out *mine*, I'll tell you that. But not to worry—I can always look for Granddad's old set up in the attic. I'm sure he had some extra transformers."

They had reached the bottom of the stairs, where daylight coming through the windows threw at least a modicum of light across the restaurant and bar. Jim stopped suddenly, turning her toward him.

"Your granddad's old set up in the attic? You're not kidding me? A nice old set tucked away up there? Darlin', will you marry me?"

It was probably, she decided, one of the strangest marriage proposals ever offered. "Yes," she said simply, and for a few minutes the two of them forgot completely about Chet.

Who, to give him credit, tactfully turned away from them with a satisfied smile and left them to it.

Marcie halfway expected Sarita to be sitting on her porch waiting for her when she got home a little later— Sarita, with that typical knowing look in her eyes.

Instead, there were—yes, there *were*—five cats lined up on the top porch step. All looking very relaxed and friendly, Big Orange sitting in the middle with innocently wide eyes.

Well. That, at last, took care of that. She really hoped that there wouldn't be any more of them coming around; five should be enough, shouldn't it?

"Welcome," she told Big Orange, and he rasped an almost silent *mrrrow* at her and closed his eyes.

For the next couple of days Marcie didn't see much of Jim. The Band-Aid approach he'd been using on the electrical problems just wouldn't do it anymore; it was major-surgery time. He had to put in new cable, new fuses and generators, and Marcie didn't know what all.

Walls came out. Fixtures came down. The emergency generator worked overtime trying to take up the slack, and Jim, working overtime, too, seemed distracted and a little growly—nice, but definitely growly—when she stopped by to see how things were going.

On the second day, he called to tell her he was closing Gentleman Jim's for three days. "So I think we should go on another picnic tomorrow," he said. The growls had disappeared; he was almost purring.

"Doesn't sound as if you're taking your work very seriously," she chided him. "A picnic doesn't rewire the restaurant."

"I hired a couple of guys to do it—got it all diagrammed out for them. And I want to spend some time with you. If it rains, we could always have the picnic in your attic."

"Why do I have this feeling that you're praying for rain?"

"I'm not. Not really. I want to spend time with you. We still have a lot of things to talk about, though of course we could talk about them even if it should rain, curled up together in that magic Morris chair."

"Mmm, lovely . . . but it sounds to me as if we wouldn't get much talking done. And there are so many things to straighten out—'' She sighed. She hadn't even said anything to Sarita or to Ellen yet. There were a hundred details to concentrate on, and she couldn't concentrate. She had new lists: Contact the school board; go back and get rid of the furniture in the apartment; try to pack up what she wanted to bring to Chennowah Grove.

And in the meantime, she hadn't made any headway at all in getting the land for the community center. Her head had been whirling ever since she backed into that transformer, and she wondered if the electrical shock might have affected her brain.

"A picnic," she told him, "would be wonderful. Somewhere secluded. I can make sandwiches and salad."

"No, thanks. We have a passel of food here at the restaurant that should be used. I'll make us up a special feed. You just bring your own sweet self—and maybe a swimsuit. I know a little secret stretch of beach near Elk Cove. I'll pick you up around ten-thirty in the morning."

Sarita was standing—splendid today in some kind of crinkly black fabric lavishly embroidered with silver—just outside her door when Marcie hung up the phone and turned. A rather solemn Sarita, looking thoughtful.

"It's all going well, then," she stated. It seemed to Marcie that Sarita should sound happier about it.

"Is something wrong?" she asked involuntarily.

Sarita seemed to shake herself, and a smile replaced the solemnity. "Oh, dear child, no. Most truths make themselves apparent with time. But not all."

Marcie frowned, trying to figure that one out.

"Be patient," Sarita told her. "I think the rest of

the threads will soon be untangled. You do handle things so well. And here, I brought you some cookies.''

But Sarita wouldn't stay for tea; she had, she said, some personal readings to do. "Be sure to remember the lights," she said cryptically, and left.

Jim wondered what Marcie would say when he told her that Kenny MacIntyre had disappeared completely—had been gone since the night of the Fourth.

"Well, I'd say," she said, spreading out the blanket on the soft grasses under a grove of maple trees, "that he just might have run away because he had a guilty conscience." She glanced up at Jim. "Wouldn't you?"

"You mean you're not suspecting foul play? You're not visualizing him as an injured innocent?"

She snorted. "After what he did to Ellen? From what you told me, it all ties in so neatly. No. I'm not feeling sorry for Kenny MacIntyre these days."

He almost told her that he was glad she'd finally seen the light, but decided that sounded too much like "I told you so," and he was learning—maybe—when to hold his tongue. "You're probably right," he said, feeling rather proud of himself for using those words.

He was rewarded with a quick smile and a peck on the cheek. "That the best you can do?" he groused, and she spent several minutes proving she could do better. Much better.

She was the one who pulled away at last and pointed out that they had a great deal of food to eat and a lot to talk about.

"Speaking of which," he said, finishing off a dill pickle that set his teeth on edge, "what was it that Wes Eddleston was talking to you about there at the Fourth of July shindig?"

"Why, were you jealous, Jim?" Then, in a tone tinged with anger, "That man is a stubborn, egotistical lech of an idiot."

"Tell me something I *don't* know," he said patiently. "Like exactly what he said."

"I think he already knew that his grandiose scheme was being turned down by a town council that was smarter than I gave it credit for. So, knowing that I wanted that land, he decided to see just how much I wanted it."

"A proposition, I take it."

"Right. As in, 'If you'd like to be nice to me, honey, I'll bet we could make a deal.' I told him to buzz off, in no uncertain terms."

"I can just hear it. You know, it would be very satisfying to feel my right fist connect with the left side of his jaw."

"I nearly did that myself. But, oh, Jim, that property would be so perfect. That old train station could be restored and built onto, and the grounds are perfect for a softball field. I could do so much with it!"

"Maybe he'll come down on the price. Could his sense of civic honor, duty, and pride be touched?"

"No way. He never heard of such things. It's all so depressing."

"It'll all work out," he said soothingly. "A little at a time. Meanwhile, come on over here, darlin', and I'll try to cheer you up."

He did, she had to admit, a magnificent job of that.

The sun was sending slantwise gleams of gold through the branches when they decided to walk beside the laughing little creek that tumbled over mossy rocks down to the lake.

This was, indeed, a secluded part of the woods that bordered Chennowah Lake; they seemed to be the only people within miles. And it was, Marcie thought, a beautiful day. "Almost like paradise, after all," she said in a low voice, stopping to watch a pair of squirrels play tag along the trunk and spreading branches of an ancient oak.

"Adam and Eve in the Garden of Eden," Jim said, then stopped, his head tilted to one side, listening intently to something she hadn't heard.

"What is it?" she began, but he hushed her, eyes scanning the thick overgrowth on the far side of the creek.

She could see nothing over there; the branches were moving slightly, but that could be the breeze, couldn't it? "What's there?" she whispered.

"The snake, I think, in the Garden," he hissed back. "Just stand real still."

She obeyed. She and Jim were half hidden behind a clump of sumac. A fleeting thought of wild things like bears and foxes and wildcats went through her head, but she didn't think there were any of those around in this day and age.

Then the bushes on the other side of the creek parted, and a very dirty face peered out, followed in short order by a somewhat bedraggled Kenny MacIntyre.

He stood stock-still, apparently having heard their movements and voices and wondering where they were. After a moment's hesitation he crept forward. A fallen tree had bridged the creek with a fat trunk. Kenny started stealthily across it, still watching the tangled undergrowth where Jim and Marcie watched unseen.

"Stay right where you are, Kenny," Jim said, stepping out of concealment. "Don't you move another inch."

"Hey, where'd you come from? What do you want, anyway? I'm not doing anything."

"Except worrying your parents to death and running away from your troubles," Jim told him.

"I didn't do anything wrong," the boy said, but Marcie was at Jim's side by now, her eyes blazing.

"If you're the one who cut holes in the canoes, you darned near killed someone," she shot at him. "I call that wrong, don't you?"

"Well, how did I know she couldn't swim? Everybody knows how to swim." Kenny looked back over his shoulder at the log, as if weighing his chances of fleeing back into the shadows on the other side of the creek.

"That was an admission of guilt, wasn't it?" Jim asked, looking at Marcie.

"Clear as day," she confirmed. "And doesn't he look the picture of guilt?"

"So what are you going to do about it? Put me in prison?"

Marcie was about to say that she didn't think it would come to that when the boy, panic obviously overriding logical thought, started toward them like a juggernaut, head down and feet pumping.

He must have thought that he could get around them by swinging five feet to the left, but Marcie sidestepped even more quickly than the boy. When he got even with her, she caught him off balance.

There was something almost graceful in the way he arced through the air, landing on his back with the air knocked out of him and an unbelieving look on his face.

A look that was mirrored on Jim's. "What on earth was that?" he asked.

"I have," Marcie said a trifle smugly, dusting her hands together, "a brown belt in judo. I always figured it might come in handy in my work and my neighborhood someday. Didn't think I'd use it in Chennowah Grove, though."

Kenny was still where she'd tossed him, obviously petrified.

"Not a black belt, for Pete's sake?"

"I'm working on that."

"I thought you didn't believe in the use of force— especially on children," Jim said almost accusingly.

"Well, there are times, aren't there, when one must make exceptions to the rules? This was one of those times."

"Geez," Kenny said in awe.

## *Chapter Ten*

Jim put on his fiercest face and looked down at the boy, who had managed to sit up but was still staring at Marcie as if he thought she might just launch him into orbit with one flip of her wrist.

"Now, are we ready to talk?" Jim asked.

"You're going to try talking? Reasoning? I thought that sort of thing didn't work with Kenny," Marcie said, only a slight tinge of sarcasm in her voice.

"That was before he saw what could happen if he crossed the wrong person the wrong way. Or the right person the wrong way. Stand up, bonehead, and let's discuss what we're going to do with you."

"Yessir," Kenny said, hauling himself to his feet, still with a wary eye on Marcie.

"Straighter," Jim directed.

Kenny squared his shoulders and looked up at Jim. "You gonna put me in jail?" he asked, a slight quaver in his voice.

"I'm not sure that's necessary—yet," Jim told him. "However, without your cooperation, I could *become* sure very quickly."

"Yessir." Kenny glanced over at Marcie. "Ma'am."

"First thing—what are you doing out here in the woods?"

"Hiding. I haven't been doing anything wrong, honest."

"Wonder what your parents would say about that. You've had them worried for the past year, and right now they've even got the sheriff's department out looking for you. You think that's smart?"

"Guess not." The boy was tracing a circle in the dust with the toe of a dirty sneaker. "Hey, I'm sorry. What are you going to do with me?"

"I'm not sure you're sorry enough, and I'm dreaming up all kinds of things to do with you." He turned to Marcie. "How does community service sound to you?"

"Pregnant with possibilities," she said.

"Okay. We start with repainting over any and all graffiti that can be found within five miles of Chennowah Grove. I don't care whether you did it or not. And doing shopping for the seniors who can't get out. And clearing the brush from the paths in the park. And—"

"And," Marcie interposed, thinking Jim's ideas were great but figuring she'd had more experience with this sort of thing than he had, "you will observe a reasonable curfew and apologize to anyone you have done any harm to, especially your parents, and when school starts, you will do everything in your power to get your grades up and keep them up. We can get help for you in that, if you want it, and you'd better want it. And you'll pick your friends with more care."

"Geez," Kenny said again. He didn't sound deliriously happy about their suggestions. Marcie took a step toward him, and he quickly took a step back. "I'll try," he said hastily.

"Doggoned if that doesn't all sound like a real good start, boy," Jim told him. "We can talk about all this later. Right now I think you'd better hightail it for home and let your folks know you're all right."

"My dad's gonna skin me," Kenny mumbled. "Are you gonna talk to him and tell him about this comm— community service thing?"

"We will," Jim promised. "I'll also promise you that if you step out of line even a little, I'll sic Miss Newberry on you again. Or Mrs. Wolverton, as the case may be when the occasion arises. You'd better hope it doesn't arise. You got the picture?" Kenny looked confused but convinced, and nodded. "Now *git,*" Jim commanded.

Kenny got.

"The whole town's going to have quite a job on its hands, getting that kid and his friends squared away," Jim said, watching the boy disappear between the trees. "Is it worth it?"

"I'm surprised at you. Of course it's worth it. You and I can do a lot together."

"I like the sound of that. But not necessarily in connection with that borderline Jesse James."

"And just what were you like at that age?" she asked innocently.

"A borderline Jesse James. Point taken. I may still even have a little of it left in me. . . . Hey, I didn't say that. You have to promise here and now that you'll never throw me over your shoulder or flip me flat on my back."

"Not unless I really feel it's necessary," she cooed

at him. "Just watch your step, cowboy. You never know what could happen next."

"Come here and console me. Your words have me shivering with fear."

When they resumed their stroll through the dusk of the woods, a quiet gentleness took control of Marcie's heart. She and Jim were working out differences rather well, thanks, and replacing antagonisms with cooperation—with love—at least for now. It wouldn't always be that way, given the fact that they both liked to be top gun, but—

"Where's that coming from?" Jim stood still suddenly, listening to a rough, grumbling roar that seemed to be gaining volume by the second. Marcie had been so lost in thought, she hadn't even noticed it.

"A car? No, sounds like a truck. But there are no roads out here, are there?"

"An old cart track, if I remember right. That's a truck. Mmm, sounds to me like about a 1957 Chevy heavy-duty pickup."

"You have talents I didn't know about," Marcie said with admiration. "What model?"

"That I'm not sure of, but you just wait until you've found out about some of the rest of my talents, ma'am."

"I can't wait." She leaned against him, and they both listened: The truck, out of sight, spluttered away from them for some distance, seemed to stop completely for a few minutes, and then choked, gasped, and ground its way to life again, gradually disappearing from their hearing.

The only sounds left were an indignantly scolding squirrel on a branch above them and a raucous crow at the top of a pine near the lake.

"Let's see if we can find the cart track," Jim said. "I'm curious."

It took only a couple of minutes to locate the bumpy, rock-strewn old road, mostly overgrown and probably almost entirely hidden from the main road just south of them.

They picked their way along it to the marshy inlet where it ended, and Marcie took one look and growled the most menacing growl Jim had heard since he'd cornered a she-bobcat back ten years or so ago.

"Old shipping boxes, oil and paint drums—someone's been using this spot for a private dump, looks like," he said disgustedly.

"Someone?" Marcie said. The growl was still apparent in her voice. "*Someone?* Take a look at the stenciled lettering on that drum over there. EOM—Eddleston Outboard Motors, maybe?"

"There's leakage too. What a stinkin' mess!"

"It certainly is. Literally." Marcie looked thoughtful. The wheels in her mind were whirling at top speed, and the gears were beginning to mesh, producing some diabolically clever ideas. "Isn't that interesting, though?" she asked musingly. "Oh, but I couldn't do that, could I?"

"Interesting's not exactly the word I'd use for it—" He stopped and gave her a sharp look. "Just what are you thinking, darlin'? Maybe something like what I'm beginning to think you're thinking?"

"Just exploring possibilities. . . ."

"I believe it's called blackmail."

"Oh, no, I wouldn't like to call it that. Just a simple marshaling of the facts and a call for fairness."

"You going to do the same thing to him you did to Kenny?" He sounded hopeful.

She chuckled. "Not quite, though it's a temptation. Let's say I hope I can throw him off balance—figuratively—and gain some very important ground. With this and the lights—"

"What lights?"

"Ah, that's another story. Sarita kept telling me they were important. I think that with them and with this mess, we have a handle on the situation, darlin'. Come on. We're going to the Eddlestons'."

He didn't argue. "I kinda liked the way you said 'darlin', darlin'," he said. "Let's go."

The streetlights had begun to glow by the time they pulled up the long driveway to the old-fashioned porte-cochere on the side of the sprawling old mansion.

Marcie's jaw was set, and she'd said little on the way to the house. "Hey, I'm glad we're on the same side, judging from the look of you," he told her.

"Mmmph," she managed. "Leave the talking to me, okay? I've got my little speech all mapped out."

"Yes, *ma'am*."

It was Wes Eddleston himself who answered the door.

"Well, now, isn't this a pleasure, Miss Newberry!" His small eyes flicked, without warmth, toward Jim, and he lost a little of his overly friendly look. "Mr. Wolverton. What brings you up here?" He didn't seem inclined to invite them into the main part of the house, so they stood in a stiff, distrustful group in the middle of the spacious entry hall.

"Several things. Mainly, a fair deal on the old railroad land," Marcie said.

"We did talk about that at the picnic, didn't we? I

had a few suggestions—'' He looked uneasily at Jim and fell silent.

"Forget your suggestions. I have a few of my own. First, Jim and I found a nasty little spot down by the lake—off Sparrow Lane; I'm sure you know where it is—that needs to be cleaned up."

"What kind of— Oh. Now, I don't know anything about whatever it is you're talking about."

"Of course you do. Your private illegal dumping site is what we're talking about. One that you could be fined very heavily for, if its location were made public. I wouldn't be surprised if the EPA wouldn't like to know something about this, for that matter."

"Good heavens. No. What I mean is, I'm sure something can be done to clean up any accidental spillage. If there is any."

"You know there is. You can start making amends by doing it on your own, right away, or I can go to the town council and any other authorities that need to be notified."

Jim looked from one to the other of them, hiding the touch of amusement that underlaid his natural disgust with the man. It was difficult to keep quiet, but Marcie was doing very well.

"All right, all right. What else do you want me to do?"

"Come down to a reasonable price on that land. We can build a great community center there, and that would be the best use I can think of for that acreage."

"Wait a minute, Miss Newberry. I'm sure I can get top dollar for that property. I'm not sure I like the way your suggestions are taking shape."

"Wait a minute yourself, Mr. Eddleston. I haven't liked the shape of some of your suggestions, either.

And there's another thing you might want to take into account, and that's the matter of the . . . ummm . . . nocturnal visitors you've been having up here when Sophie's been gone."

He actually spluttered. "Visi— Why, I've had some business associates up here, that's all!"

"Monkey business," Jim murmured under his breath, but Wes caught the words and turned red. "I think I'd take Marcie's words pretty seriously, Wes," Jim suggested.

"I can't see how I can drop the price as much as you'd want," he blustered. "Not when real estate prices are escalating the way they have been."

"Oh, yes, you can, dear." The quiet voice came from the arched entry to the living room on the right. Sophie, quiet and straight, seemed to materialize in the doorway, her arms folded in front of her and her gray eyes nailing her husband to the wall. "You can drop the price substantially. I think it would be an excellent idea to do so."

"Sophie, this is none of your business!" Wes Eddleston had turned a very unbecoming shade that resembled raw liver. But he couldn't quite look directly at his wife.

"Wes, it *is* my business. Eddleston Outboard Motors is my business—fifty-one percent of it is—if you'll remember the details of my father's will." She glanced at Jim and Marcie, who looked a little lost at this turn of events. "It used to be Acme Outboards, before Daddy died and Wes took over. My family's business. But that was years ago. . . ."

Something stirred in Marcie's memory. Yes, when she'd been small, there had been the big Acme billboard outside town. . . .

Guilt warred with triumph in Marcie's mind. She hadn't planned on hurting Sophie in any way, hadn't known she was there. "I'm sorry, Mrs. Eddleston," she said inadequately.

"Oh, I'm not, dear," Sophie told her. "I've had time to think, there at Lottie's bedside, talking about the important things of life, and I've come to the conclusion that there are some fundamental changes that need to be made in this house."

Wes opened his mouth to say something and apparently thought better of it. Marcie had a suspicion that was the first time anything like that had happened in a long time.

"I think," Sophie said graciously, "that we should all go into the library and have a nice glass of sherry and talk about all this. It's time Wes contributed something to the well-being of Chennowah Grove, began thinking in a more civic-minded way."

"But the money—" he started.

"Think of the tax write-off possibilities, if nothing else," Sophie told him coolly. "Right this way, if you don't mind. I'd like to get to know you two young people a lot better. You're engaged, are you?"

"What is she, another Sarita?" Jim whispered in Marcie's ear as they dutifully followed Sophie and a reluctant Wes into the beautifully spacious library. "I haven't even given you a ring yet."

"Just see to it that you do it soon," she whispered back at him. "I certainly wouldn't want to disappoint Sophie and Sarita. It appears that could be dangerous."

Days later, as the dust settled, Marcie was able to cross any number of things—very important things—off her lists.

She thanked Big Orange for causing fights and getting her up in the middle of the night to watch the clandestine lights at the Eddlestons'.

She thanked Sophie for her help in clearing the way for the purchase of the property.

She thanked Sarita for telling her the lights were important.

And she thanked Jim—most fulsomely—for the beautiful diamond-and-sapphire engagement ring that now glittered on her left hand. "Shucks, ma'am, I just thought those li'l blue stones would match your eyes," he said with mock humility.

"So, your plans are all made." Sarita poured iced herbal tea for the three of them a few evenings later in her big, homey kitchen, pattering back and forth across the floor in her bare feet with her jungle-print muumuu billowing around her. A soft rain had fallen during the late afternoon, and Chennowah Grove seemed washed clean, more vividly green than usual. "Everything's settled."

"I wouldn't say that, exactly," Marcie said, feeling contrary. "There are still a lot of loose ends to clear up, and there's a lot of work ahead. Thank goodness Jim has the experience to supervise the reconstruction at the train station."

"We're putting a train museum in there—did we tell you?" he asked Sarita. "And extensions on the back, and building another building on the west side."

"And Kenny has promised to try to behave," Marcie put in. "That's a relief."

"We'll see that he does," Jim said darkly.

"I suppose most people have problems and bad decisions in their past," Sarita said, looking through them and beyond them as if seeing another time, another place. "Sometimes difficult episodes in childhood, sometimes when we're older. If we're lucky, we all grow past them." Neither Jim nor Marcie could disagree with that, and there was a moment's silence while they thought about it. "I know that you're glad to come back to a place that you always loved—but do you think you'll miss teaching, Marcie?"

"Probably," she admitted. "But it looks as if I'll be taking on the whole job of coordinating and directing activities at the center, once it's done. And I'll help Jim out at the restaurant when he needs it."

"Actually, I was thinking of putting her up for mayor in the next election," Jim said. "No way she could lose."

"I'll take it under consideration," Marcie said seriously. "I hadn't thought about it, but it might be a good idea."

"I don't need to consult the cards to know you'd win," Sarita told her. "And since the two of you will be staying in your grandmother's house, I'd be living next door to the mayor. I'd like that, I think. There's a certain amount of prestige to it."

"You're getting too far ahead of me, Sarita. Besides, isn't there some kind of a law against the mayor of a town being mother-henned by the local herbalist?"

Sarita had risen to get more ice and stood for a moment, looking dreamily out of her kitchen window, ice tray in hand. Jim followed her over to the counter to put more cookies on the plate. "Oh, I don't know. You need it, I think," Sarita said. "You and Jim both. He's missed having a mother all these years, haven't you, Jim?"

A curious silence followed her question. Marcie looked up at the two of them, standing there silhouetted

against the twilight that was growing silvery-damp beyond the window, staring almost eye to eye in the
stillness.

"You do seem to know everything, Sarita," Jim
said at last.

"Not quite." Sarita headed serenely back to the table
with the ice. "But I'm working on it."

Lightning bugs were rising from grass still beaded
with raindrops when Jim and Marcie made their way
back through the gap in the lilac hedge to the cottage.
It had to be the light, Marcie thought, glowing low
through the clouds now, that made everything seem so
vibrant. It was almost like magic. A special kind of
magic. "Perfect," she murmured.

"Your own special paradise?" Jim asked, teasing.

"Mmm. Lost and regained."

He thought he understood, and he figured she was
right, at that. He slipped his arm around her, and they
walked slowly, savoring the evening, up the brick path
that led to Gram's cottage. *Their* cottage.

They were met midway up the path by five sleek,
well-fed, complacent-looking cats that followed them
silently into the cottage.

*Their* cottage.

WATERLOO HIGH SCHOOL LIBRARY
1464 INDUSTRY RD.
ATWATER, OHIO 44201

WATERLOO HIGH SCHOOL LIBRARY
1464 INDUSTRY RD.
ATWATER. OHIO 44201

Somewhere near paradise                    14208
Everitt, Marjorie                          F  Eve